THE OTHER REALM

I0520072

Deatri King-Bey

King-Bey Productions

This is a work of fiction. All the characters, events, incidents, names, organizations and places portrayed in this novel are either products of the author's imagination or are used fictitiously. Any resemblance to actual persons, living or dead, business establishments, events or locales is entirely coincidental.

The Other Realm Copyright 2010 by Deatri King-Bey
ISBN-13:978-0615972176 (King-Bey Productions)
ISBN-10:0615972179

Cover Artist: Deatri King-Bey
Editor: Lynel Johnson Washington
Proof Reader: Paulette Nunlee

Visit Deatri online http://DeatriKingBey.com

ACKNOWLEDGMENTS

I'd like to thank God for giving me a vivid imagination and a love of world building. I thank my friends and family for always supporting me. And I thank the readers for taking chances with my genre hopping. Thank you for sticking with me and spreading the word about my work.

DEATRI'S TITLES

Romance

Beauty and the Beast

Broken Promises

Christmas Angel (Second Chances)

Diamond in the Rough

Ebony Angel

If You Only Knew

Love's Desire (Free Read)

Journey's End

Santa's Helper (Write Brothers Series Book II)

Silk Scarves and Apples (Second Chances)

Tease (Write Brothers Series Book IV)

Tell Her How You Feel (Write Brothers Series Book I)

The Drama The Street and the Seduction (Free Read)

The Only Option (Second Chances)

The Other Realm

Third Time's A Charm (Write Brothers Series Book III)

Trapped In Paradise (Free Read)

Whisper Something Sweet

Women's Fiction

Caught Up

Jodie's Choice

Operation White Rose

Picture Perfect

Suspense (as L. L. Reaper)

Black Widow and the Sandman

Hell Hath No Fury

Birth of the Black Widow (Free Read)

The Sandman Cometh (Free Read)

Nonfiction

Become A Successful Author

CHAPTER ONE

Majestic bird should be reserved for eagles and hawks, thought Aurora. *Eagles, hawks, and now geese.* She watched a goose soar across the courtyard, his wings fully expanded. In a few graceful strokes, he traveled two hundred yards and descended into an effortless landing.

She'd never seen anything so magnificent. The goose took her mind back to her pet goose that flew away one day, never to return. She constantly worried about what became of him.

As if the goose knew of his audience, he took off again, skimmed the freshly mowed grounds, then stopped in front of her.

She quickly checked over her shoulders. A few people were walking along the path that circled the office courtyard, but none were within earshot. "If I didn't know better, I'd think you were putting a show on for me," she quipped.

Aurora.

She jumped and clinched her pounding chest at the sound of a deep, husky voice calling her name. She couldn't tell what direction it came from, but she'd never heard a more clear sound. After a quick visual scan of the area, she took out her imitation hearing aids to see if she'd actually heard speaking.

She'd had the earplugs made in the shape of hearing aids to block out the distorted sounds she heard instead of clear voices.

Aurora.

Her heart lurched forward from an anxiety-laced adrenaline rush. One of her earplugs slipped out of her hand. She knelt to pick it up. The goose stepped forward and stood on the device.

Aurora.

1

She looked around again. There was no one around. Not even on the walking path. She and the goose were the only warm-blooded creatures in sight. "Please, mister goose," she murmured. "I think I'm losing my mind and," she pointed at his foot, "I need my earplug." He didn't move.

You're not crazy. It's me—Tahlan, the voice explained.

She sat on her haunches and fought to remain in control over her nerves. "Oh great. Now the voice in my head has a name."

A hearty chuckle filled her head. *I haven't heard sarcasm in such a long time. Come to think of it, I haven't heard spoken word in such a long time.*

She slowly rose. "I'm hearing voices, a goose is standing on my earplug and I'm talking to myself." She held out her hands. "What next?"

This goose is the voice in your head.

Her lips pursed and eyes scrunched. "Oh yeah, I'm crazy. Now the goose is talking to me." She spotted a few people across the lawn walking onto the path. "Listen here, mister goose. Geese do not talk," she whispered with a touch of agitation.

I know this all sounds crazy, Aurora, but please listen to me. I'm the voice in your head.

She crossed her arms over her chest. "If you're talking to me, why isn't your mouth moving? And how can I understand you?" She held out her imitation hearing aid. External sounds were distorted for her. Therefore, she couldn't understand spoken word. "I'm not happy about it, but I'm crazy. I'm either hearing voices that don't exist, or I think a goose is talking to me. Either way, I need some serious psychological help."

My mouth isn t moving because geese don t talk.

She laughed so hard she drew the attention of the people who walked along the path.

After she calmed, he continued, *I don t have lips in this form. We communicate to each other telepathically.*

"Not only am I fighting with a goose, but I'm losing the argument. This isn't right." She walked away. "Keep it. I'll have another made," she said over her shoulder. Audiologist never found a medical reason why Aurora's hearing was distorted. She wore the imitation hearing aids to block out the noise and to minimize questions from people. It was much easier just saying she was hard of hearing than explaining the truth.

Aurora. The goose bent his long neck down, picked up her earplug, then gave chase. *Listen to me.*

"I don't argue with animals. I'm going through some sort of crazy, think–geese–speak psychosis thing."

You have a clear mind and heart. You know you re not crazy.

"Crazy people never believe they're crazy."

He stepped in front of her.

She stumbled over him onto the cement walking path. "Listen up you crazy goose." She glared into his beady black eyes, and a jolt of recognition zipped through her. It took a bit, but she shook it off.

"If you trip me one more 'gin, I'll pluck your feathers and have you for dinner."

He dropped the earplug onto her lap. *I find your spoken word comforting, but you don t have to open your mouth. Just think to me. Tell me to do a flying trick. You ll see this is real.*

She wiped her hearing aid off with her denim shirt. "Yuck. Goose slob."

Please try. This is important. What do you have to lose?

"My mind. But I'll try anyway." She closed her eyes and imagined the goose sailing a few feet above ground. She opened her eyes and watched him glide a few feet above the ground.

She changed her thoughts to him circling the flagpole. He circled the flagpole.

Her whole body trembled. "Oh no. This can't be." She ran into the building and practically knocked over a few innocent bystanders who'd come out to enjoy the show.

~~~~~~

Aurora sat across from the therapist and fidgeted with one of the throw pillows from the couch. "You can't tell anyone what I say in here, right?" She peeked up momentarily.

"What is said in our sessions is confidential."

"Good, because I have a real doosie." She watched Dr. Price out of the corner of her eye.

He stifled his grin. "Doosie, huh? Why don't you tell me what this is about?" He hated to admit it, but the way she kept watching his mouth aroused him. They were both in their early thirties, but he

4

wouldn't consider dating a patient, especially a delusional one.

"I was sitting in the courtyard watching this goose when he started a conversation with me." She leaned forward and rested her elbows on her knees. "I'm not talking about honking. He actually spoke to me. The really scary part is—I kept answering."

He scribbled, *patient hears voices of animals speaking to her. Geese in particular.* "Have any other animals spoken to you?"

She burst into a belly-tightening, tear-jerking laugh. "I'm sorry, but this sounds too crazy. And you asked with such a straight face. Whew." In an attempt to catch her breath, she snorted. "I'm a pure 'D' nut."

"I don't think you're crazy."

"I talk to geese and they answer. That's crazy." She stood "This was a waste of time. I shouldn't have come. It's not like he told me to kill anyone."

"Please sit. I can tell this episode has scared you. You were brave enough to call for help. Now be brave enough to accept it." He felt sorry for her. She was sane, yet knew her delusions would lead her into insanity. She didn't know how to fight, but he could help her.

She returned to her seat. "Geese don't talk."

"No, they don't," he reassured. "Do you know of anyone in your family who suffers from delusions?"

"I'm an orphan. Maybe my biological mom was some sort of paranoid schizophrenic."

He jotted, *hides pain and fear behind jokes and laughter. Orphan.* "What did the goose tell you?"

"His name is Tahlan, and it's important that I listen to him."

"Why is it important for you to listen to him?"

"I don't know. I was trippin' over a goose talking and didn't think to ask."

He stifled a grin. "Where is the name Tahlan from?"

"You got me. I'd never heard of it before."

"Did anything else stand out to you?"

"Besides a goose speaking to me using telepathy, I'd say his voice. I've never heard a clear voice other than my own thoughts and dreams. Even my dreams are muffled. I didn't realize that until I heard Tahlan. I can hear him perfectly, and he feels familiar."

"I'm sorry. I wasn't aware."

"External sounds are garbled messes to me." She took out one of her imitation hearing aids. "They make these things so small now days. I'm great at reading lips and was taught to speak as a child. I'll bet I sound like my instructor." She focused on everything in the small office except Dr. Price. "She made me repeat the same thing over and over again until I sounded right to her. Formed my mouth correctly. I'm talking every word. Every phrase." She twiddled her fingers. "Yeah, I'll bet I sound like her…"

He allowed her to ramble off her nervous energy a while longer. "Tell me about the voice."

She closed her eyes. "His voice was rich, deep and filled me with this odd warmth. You see, I've always had a chill, but it comes from within. I can wear a full-length mink in the middle of a Texas August and still feel this chill. Somehow, the voice removed the chill. Or maybe it was, somehow, Tahlan. I don't know."

He waited on her to look at him so he could ask an additional question, but she kept her eyes closed and remained silent. He documented her reaction to the voice and the far off air her voice took when she spoke about it.

He tapped her knee with his mechanical pencil to draw her attention. "Was there actually a goose there?"

"Yes. I dropped my ear piece, and he handed it to me."

"A goose *handed* a hearing aid to you?"

"I have witnesses to that part," she added quickly.

He scanned his notes. "Did you grow up in a group home, foster home, or were you adopted."

She stiffened. "What does that have to do with talking geese?"

"The more I know about your background, the more I'll be able to help."

7

"I was adopted by a church. I became a mascot of sorts. So how do I make the voice stop? I'm already addicted to it. I want to hear it. Feel the warmth again. Even duck boy has grown on me. This can't be good."

"It will take time."

Her posture drooped, and she slouched back on the tweed couch.

He took out his appointment book. "We need to meet at least twice a week. I have Monday and Thursdays open from five to six."

"I guess that works for me." She input the information into her cell phone.

He waited for her to look at him. "I want you to keep a catalogue of the voices you're hearing. Give as much detail as you can with each instance. I'm talking time, what the conversation is about, who is speaking and such. I need to do a little research of my own. We'll compare notes when we meet Thursday."

"Sounds like a plan to me." She stood to leave.

He reached into his pocket, pulled out his wallet, then handed her his card. "This has my home and work phones. If you need me, call. We'll work through this together."

After he showed her out, he finished his notes. *Mascot—a symbol of luck, oftentimes an animal. Possible projection onto the goose referred to as Tahlan. Though a naturally outgoing person, Aurora withdraws when she speaks of her childhood.*

CHAPTER TWO

Aurora sat cross-legged on the floor and stared at Tahlan.

He pecked at the sliding door with his bill. *You might as well let me in.*

"I'm not talking to you."

You can t close your mind to me. I heard that.

"You make me sick." She kicked at the door. "Why are you doing this to me?"

He waddled from one end of the balcony to the other. *I don t fully understand myself. I know I m in a goose body, but I m not a goose. I m a man.*

"This is stupid." She yanked the sliding door open. "I can't believe I'm following the orders of a goose. And you'd best not leave anything on my carpet."

I m house broken, he teased and followed her through the small kitchen into the living room. He stopped abruptly. *Where did you get those?* He nodded toward the framed posters on the living room walls.

"I drew them," she boasted. "They're of the world I created for my video game." She pointed to each character. "I modeled the sorceress after myself and the warrior after the man of my dreams." She glanced down at the goose. "No man actually looks like this." She returned her gaze to the fine specimen of man she'd drawn. "But hey, it's my fantasy, so everyone else has to deal with it."

What is that world?

"I call it 'The Other Realm.' It looks like a cross between Medieval Times and the Wild, Wild West, but it has wizards, elves, dragons and stuff." Her eyes opened wide, and her fingers flailed. "You know, fannnn-tasy."

I don t know what Medieval, Wild, Wild West or fannnn-tasy are.

"Don't worry about it. The warrior and sorceress work through different levels, kicking butt and growing more powerful so they can defeat Prophious."

Prophious?

She knew it was silly, but she always imagined The Other Realm as her true home. There she fit in. There is where her real family was, and the warrior would someday be her husband.

"He's an evil man. He murdered the true rulers of The Other Realm and..."

We belong there.

"Excuse you." She loved talking about her world, and he'd cut her off mid-sentence. She laughed internally, wondering how she expected a goose to have manners.

We belong there. That s our home.

Not ready to give in to the insanity, she pointed at the pictures. "Those are images based on my dreams, not real. Oh my. Listen to me telling a goose other realms don't exist." She shook her head. "So tell me, Tahlan. What makes you think we belong there?"

I didn t start remembering anything until a few weeks ago. Before then I just traveled. I was searching. For what, I don t know. Then I remembered being hatched. You were the first person I saw.

"You're the abandoned goose egg I found! Wow! You grew into a great specimen of goose." She winked. "The only pet you can have in this building is fish. Someone ratted me out to the condo association, and you had to go." She remembered the day she gave him away. As long as she had the goose, her inner chill had decreased. She visited him regularly, then one day his handlers said he'd flown away. The full chill returned that same day.

Once my memory returned, I found others from there. He nodded his bill toward the posters. *We all need to return. You re the only one who can help us. We ve all crossed over as animals and can t open the portal.*

She held up her hands. "Wait one cotton-picking second. Are you saying there are other animals that talk? This is ridiculous. And I'm not an animal. What makes you think I come from your realm?"

Because I can communicate with you. Because you ve drawn our home. You just don t remember yet, but you will. You were born human and taught not to believe. This world is strange to me. I don t understand it. Look at your drawings. That s our world, Aurora, he said with a passion she felt in her heart. *I know you feel it.*

She stared at the images of elves, dragons, sorcerers and warriors. The Other Realm was somehow a part of her, always revealing itself in

11

dreams. If she crossed over, maybe she could find her warrior. "How did you know my name?"

I was drawn to you. When my memories returned, I knew your name. Haven t you always felt out of place here? I didn t fit in with the other geese.

A deep belly laugh bent her over.

You laugh a lot.

"Don't get me wrong." She wiped the tears of laughter from her eyes. "I could listen to you speak all day. The closest I've come to hearing someone speak clearly was a hushed female voice in my dreams. This is hilarious." She sat on the sofa. "Think about it. The people of The Other Realm have no idea this realm exists. If you were living there, and one day a grasshopper came to you and started a conversation about other realms…" She shrugged.

His hearty laugh filled her heart. *I see your point.*

"So what do you need from me?"

Since you re the only human, you re the only one who can open the portal. Once you open the portal, we ll all go home.

"But since I'm the only human, does that mean I'm an animal on the other side? Like a familiar or something. If so, no thanks. I'm no one's pet. I'll stay here. My games have consistently been on several top-ten lists for years. I have it good here." She slouched back on the suede couch.

I don t know, but you must return with us. You don t belong here.

"I'll open the portal for you, but I'm not stepping through and turning into a goat or some crazy mess like that. Shoot, forget that."

Aurora.

She leaned forward, lowered her brows and stared down into his beady, black eyes.

"Listen here, duck boy. I don't want to be a goat, duck, or anything except human. I can't believe I even considered the word of a duck."

He hopped onto the coffee table and stretched his long neck forward. *First and foremost, I am not a duck! I'm a goose. Secondly, our home is in trouble, and we are needed. We do not belong here, Aurora!*

For the past few weeks, she'd felt an urgency to return to The Other Realm, but that was impossible. Now a goose stood on her coffee table insisting it was possible. She could go to the place that had always felt like her home. She just couldn't let go of the way of life she knew for the unknown. "Why am I needed?"

I don't know. He relaxed. *In all honesty, I can't remember. I'm running on instinct. All I know is we must return. I was to find us and the portal.*

"This is so much to digest." She stared at the large goose that was standing on her coffee table: flesh, bones, and feathers. "I'm not crazy, am I? This is real."

Yes, it is real. This is crazy to me also. Look at me. He spread his wings. *I'm a goose.*

"Your wingspan is amazing. I'd never given geese a second thought until I found you a few years ago. They're truly beautiful creatures to watch fly."

I can t remember what it feels like being human. I can t imagine anything feeling as great as flying. Flying is literally part of me.

"I'm afraid of heights. I never want to fly." She looked at the image of the dark, powerful warrior, then Tahlan. His voice and personality would fit the warrior perfectly. She shrugged it off. The Other Realm and its creatures existed, but the characters of the game were not real. They were based off the reality. "That's my home, our home."

Yes.

She drew in a deep breath and released it slowly. "I guess it's time for us to go home." If she didn't know better, she'd swear the goose smiled. "How far away are the others?"

Close. We were all put in the same town. Tomorrow we have to see Lamir. He s been here for over forty years. I think he knows everything. He guided me to the portal.

"Well I need some sleep." She went into her bedroom. "Where is this Lamir, and what's his story?" She flipped on the light, crossed over to her dresser and sorted through her drawers.

Tahlan hopped onto the bed. *Your walls...* he trailed off. They were covered with sketches of The Other Realm. She looked around and saw him examine the images above her headboard.

Who is this?

She'd drawn several images of herself at various ages. Each time there was a man in the picture. He was always turned in ways you couldn't see his face.

"My adoptive parents never gave me the attention I needed, but in my dreams I had a father who loved me. That's him."

Why don t you show his face?

"No matter how hard I tried, I could never remember his face. I'd set the alarm to wake me in the middle of the night, hoping his face would be fresh so I could draw it." She shrugged. "It didn't work. I guess the important thing was I remember the love."

I thought the only voice you heard was female.

"It was. The man I think is my father didn't speak. I guess he's mute. I want to find him." She'd never felt an attachment to the female. She didn't seem as real as the man.

We shall. What are the idols for? He motioned toward her dressers.

She picked up one of her many gymnastics awards and gave him a closer look. "These aren't idols, but trophies. My parents adopted me as a show toy. Adopting a special needs child reflected well on them in the church. When in public, they'd dress me up and show me off. At home, they barely looked at me. They'd sign me up for activities at the recreation center to get rid of me." She held up a trophy. "Turns out I'm a great athlete."

What s an athlete?

15

"It's not important. Let's just say that every time I won a trophy, earned a new belt or placed in a contest, my folks were there for the photo opportunity, playing the proud parents. We looked like the perfect family, and they looked like the perfect parents." She replaced the trophy. "Enough of this. Where's Lamir?"

He's at that zoo place where you left me. He followed her into the bathroom. *Lamir is very wise. I feel we must do as he says.*

She turned on the shower.

How did you make it rain inside? He hopped into the tub. *The water is getting hot. What kind of magic is this?*

She stripped. "Get out of my shower, duck boy. This isn't magic. It's technology. Water is stored in the basement, heated up and pumped up here for me to clean myself."

He flapped his wings a few times and allowed the water to hit his chest and under feathers. *This world is completely different than our world.*

"Get out. Dang, you're rude." He hopped out. She stepped in and closed the shower curtain. "Now back to doing as Lamir says." Her words echoed off the tiled walls.

No need to yell. We have a link. Just think to me.

"I forgot. This is going to take a little getting used to. Do you always follow your instinct? How do you know he isn't trying to trick us or something?"

For now, all I have is instinct.

She dropped her head back and allowed the water to soak through her long, thick hair.

When she was a child, her adoptive mother would relax it, saying her hair had more naps than the good Lord allowed. As soon as Aurora reached eighteen, she never allowed another chemical to touch her hair. She even used all natural hair care products. "When does your instinct say we'll be leaving? I'll need to make arrangements." She grabbed the shampoo, squeezed a small dab into her hand and washed her two-strand twisted hair. She'd learned years ago that it was much easier to manage her hair if she washed it while it was braided or twisted. "Stand on that towel out there. I don't want you messing the floor."

Tomorrow will be our last day in this realm. I ll tell you everything I know tonight.

"Great. Can you understand what other people are saying or just me?"

I can t understand anyone from this realm. It all sounds like a bunch of garbled noise to me.

"Me, too." She took the jasmine scented shower gel, squeezed a bit onto the mesh sponge and washed herself. "My parents had my first set of imitation hearing aids made when I was around five. They were huge, but blocked out the noise, so I didn't mind. I think my parents wanted to announce to the world they had a special needs child. I love hearing clearly. I'm still trippin' from hearing such a powerful voice from a goose, but don't stop. You can talk all night and day if you want. I promise not to complain."

Wait until you hear Lamir. The first time I heard his voice, I just about jumped out of my feathers. I hadn t heard anyone in years, and then came this gigantic boom of a voice.

She turned off the shower. "Thanks for the warning."

Aurora hadn't intended on staying up the whole night, but she and Tahlan couldn't stop talking. She felt like she was catching up with an old friend. They discussed everything from his adventures as a goose to how she always felt like an outsider.

"The sun's rising." She grabbed her pillow. "I'd best catch a few hours sleep, but I have one more question."

You need to give up this idea of sleeping. It obviously isn t working.

"Yeah, yeah, yeah. Do you feel cold all the time? Not from the temperature outside, but from something within."

I m always hot. He paused. *That is, until I came around you.*

"This is getting weirder by the second."

CHAPTER THREE

Aurora opened the door of her spotless sports utility vehicle. "Do you want to ride with me, Tahlan?" She popped in her imitation hearing aids.

And pass up the chance to fly? No way. When we cross over to the other realm, I may never get to fly again.

"Are you sure you're human and not a dragon? Your voice is awfully powerful."

I'm certain I'm human.

She eased behind the wheel and looked down at her feathered friend. "You're giving up a lot to return to the unknown." She'd been a loner her whole life, unable to make normal attachments. Then she found the goose egg. When it hatched, her world changed. She laughed at herself with thoughts of her best friend being a bird.

So are you.

"I guess we're both crazy." She shut the door, started the engine and drove off. She'd always felt as if the world was make believe, and she was somehow stuck in a story that wasn't hers. But she was born and raised in this realm and taught this was her only reality. She made the best of it, and according to most, became a success.

Books, drawings, and games inspired by her visions of the other realm made her a very wealthy person. Yet she still felt empty inside. She glanced out the windshield and saw Tahlan soar across the sky. A sense of peace overcame her.

Unable to believe she was about to jump into the pit of the unknown with a goose, and it seemed completely normal, she smiled.

Well, if I'm a nut, I might as well go all out. She pulled into the parking lot of the zoo and parked, then walked along the brick path to the entrance.

Hatch's city zoo was one of the main tourist attractions in the small town. Though the zoo was quaint, it also had an excellent park, picnic area, rock gardens, oriental gardens, flower gardens and a children's museum. The zoo's out of the way location, on the edge of the lake, added to its beauty.

Tahlan called to Aurora. She spotted him standing in the middle of a gaggle of geese, looking like he was the head of a lion pride. "So which one's Lamir?"

You may wish to stop speaking aloud. You don't want to draw unwanted attention to yourself.

"Oopps." She covered her mouth and peeked over her shoulder to see who saw her speaking to the geese. "My bad."

He nodded toward the zoo. *He isn't a goose. He lives inside. Could you do me a favor and not allow anyone to touch me?*

"Sure. Lead the way."

The opening-time zoo crowd was minimal. The few employees who saw the pair stared and pointed, but left them alone. Many recognized her from when she used to visit her pet goose regularly.

"I hope the ice cream stand opens soon." She ran along the brick path to a neighboring exhibit. "Oh look at the spider monkey," she cooed. "Isn't he the cutest thing?"

He looks like he bites to me. We don t have tiny ones like these back home. We don t have a lot of the creatures in this zoo.

"Well in this realm we don't have sorcerers, gnomes, elves, dragons, or fairies; so I guess it all equals out. Are you positive you're not a dragon in the other realm?"

They walked toward the aviary. *My only memories of the other realm are from ground level.*

The sorrow-filled longing in his voice touched her. She didn't know what to say or how to comfort him, so she remained silent.

Instead of touring the zoo, we need to see Lamir. He waddled past the aviary entrance and continued down the walk. *Lamir is magic. Maybe you were right when you said you re his familiar.*

"I didn't say I was his familiar. I said I don't want to be a familiar. There's a major difference. Do you think he's a sorcerer?"

I m not sure. Either that or maybe an elf. They re also mystical creatures with strong magic.

She recognized the area of the zoo they were in and took off running. "I'll be right back. I've got to see if they still have my favorite exhibit."

She stopped at the fence of the alligator habitat and marveled at the giant gator. A few seconds later, Tahlan stood beside her.

This is your favorite exhibit?

"Yep." She motioned toward the alligator lying in a small pool of murky water, surrounded by vegetation. "At twenty-four feet, this here happens to be one of the largest gators in captivity. Look at him.

21

How can anything so big practically be invisible? If I didn't know what I was looking at, I'd have missed him. I'll bet tons of people walk by thinking they got rid of this exhibit."

I ll bet you re right. He flew over the fence and landed on the giant gator's back.

Panic raced through her veins. She pulled at the fence in frustration. "What are you doing, you silly goose? He'll eat you for breakfast. Get back out here now!" She stomped.

Calm down. He walked along the gator's back from tail to head.

Her heart thumped loudly in her ears. "I know you think you're king of the jungle, but you're a goose. Get your feather butt out here now!"

One of the zoo employees came running. She'd noticed him following her from a distance when she entered the zoo with Tahlan.

"We just fed him this morning, ma'am. If your goose doesn't get too close his..."

Tahlan honked several times. The alligator exited the pool and walked toward the fence.

The zoo employee's eyes opened wide in shock. "Oh man. I wish I had my camera." He stood still and watched for a few seconds, then ran off.

Aurora stared into the raven eyes of the gator and fell into a trance. The very tips of her fingers and toes warmed. The warmth radiated through her body and intensified into a raging inferno. She struggled to inhale the cool July air, but it did little to soothe.

Her ears picked up a new sound. Rushing. Clear sounds were so novel to her she had difficulty placing it. Fire. She could feel liquid fire rush through her veins. She shook her head.

Not her veins, their veins. Her mind spun with images of molten lava flowing slowly down a volcano in the middle of the forest.

"Ma'am." The worker touched her sweaty forehead with his hand. The Texas heat was hot, but at nine in the morning it was only eighty-five degrees outside. Burned by her skin, he jerked his hand back. "What the?" He shook his hand.

Dazed, Aurora looked through the man. "Who are you?"

"Don't move. I'm calling an ambulance."

Aurora, snap out of it. Tahlan hopped over the fence and poked her in the thigh with his bill.

She shook her head. "What happened?" She wiped the moisture from her brow. "Why am I sweating like a pig?"

Our bond is fire, Lamir's baritone voice boomed.

Aurora thought her mind would explode. She dropped to the ground and held her hands behind her head. Squeezing her head between her arms, she cried, "Stop!"

I'm sorry, Aurora, but you will become accustomed to my voice in a few seconds. Accept it. Just as you did the fire. Don t fight.

She wept. "Stop talking to me. It hurts. You're too loud."

Then stop listening to my voice and feel it. Like you have your whole life. You feel me, just as you did the fire. We have a bond.

The pain slowly subsided as she drew in and exhaled several deep breaths. She wiped herself off and sat up. "You're Lamir?" Somehow squinting seemed to decrease the ringing in her ears.

Yes, I am Lamir. We have not much time. Are you in too much pain to remember what I tell you?

"Actually, I'm feeling much better already. I'm at about eighty-five percent." She stood upright and scanned the area. "We're about to have company. I think that man said something about an ambulance."

Then I will make this fast. You and Tahlan must return tonight, then we will go to the portal and return home.

Ordering her thoughts, she bit on her inner jaw. "You do realize that you are..." she hunched her shoulders, then threw out her arms, "huge! How in the heck am I supposed to take you to any portal? Do you think they sell giant alligator leashes in the gift shop?"

Tahlan and Lamir laughed.

"I'm not seeing the joke in this." Fully recovered, she shifted her weight between her feet. "First he tries to drive me crazy, then you try to burn me up, you try to blow off my head and now you want to get me sent to jail."

The humans come, Lamir said.

She glanced over her shoulder and saw two paramedics rush down the curved walkway with a stretcher. "Give me a few seconds." She met the paramedics and the zoo employee halfway down the brick path. "Is there something wrong?"

"Hell yeah! You were burning up." The zoo employee held up his blistered palm. "I thought you were doing one of those spontaneous combustion things."

"Thank you for your concern. I'm feeling much better now."

"If you literally became hot enough to blister his hand, you need to be admitted into the hospital for tests," a short, balding paramedic commented.

"She burned the hell out of me. And her eyes weren't human. She came in with that goose over there. Something ain't right. Take her to the hospital before she hurts someone."

"I didn't touch you. You touched me. I'm not a danger to anyone. If I don't want to go to the hospital, I don't have to. I suggest you go and have your hand looked at. I'd hate for an infection to set in. Good day, gentlemen." She nodded, then returned to the exhibit.

They're staring, Tahlan said. *I wish I could understand what they're saying. Is Aurora your familiar?*

"I'm no one's pet, Tahlan." If she didn't know better, she would swear his bill curled into a smile.

I do not have a familiar, Lamir clarified.

Well that narrows it a bit for you, Aurora. We can return tonight after the zoo closes for Lamir and that slob of a creature over there. He flapped his wing toward a different exhibit.

Aurora glanced in the direction Tahlan motioned. "The raccoon is from the other realm, too?"

Yeah, but he doesn t talk. I can t figure him out.

So he s a raccoon. I don t think we have those in the other realm, Tahlan stated.

A lanky paramedic stood beside Aurora. "You should come with us."

She grimaced as she took out her slightly melted imitation hearing aids, then handed them to the paramedic and concentrated on Lamir and Tahlan. *Who are we, Lamir,* she thought. She felt an odd kinship with Lamir.

Once we cross over, we will be ourselves again. Tahlan is human, and the raccoon is his war horse.

Tahlan laughed. *That fat hunk of flesh is not a war horse.*

Stop being rude, duck boy. What about me, Lamir? What am I?

You are Aurora. The dawn of a new day.

She released a big sigh of relief. *Then I m me.*

She glanced at the man beside her. "Why are you still here?"

The paramedic dropped the deformed hearing aids into his shirt pocket and yelled. "Ma'am, please come with us." He held his hand out to her.

She wanted to tell him to stop yelling into her face, but instead focused on Lamir.

"Harry," the paramedic called over his shoulder. "Bring the stretcher. Something's wrong."

"Don't touch her or you'll be sorry," the burned zoo employee shouted.

Aurora could hear and couldn't understand what the men were saying, but recognized the agitation in their voices.

Lamir, we don t have much time. What are you?

And I am a dragon.

Her mouth dropped open. *But dragons don t even exist in the other realm. They were all killed.*

Not all of us. I could give you visions of the other realm, Caiaphas, but your subconscious interfered at times. Your visions of Caiaphas are not all factual.

Aurora continued, *When I was two, maybe three, I started having dreams about the other realm. I mean Caiaphas. I remember this soft-spoken woman who kept speaking to me in my dreams.*

She was my mother, Lamir answered. *I knew my voice would terrify you, and I needed for you to learn to speak.*

She frowned. *Your mother was human?*

Yes. I do not have time to explain everything to you now. There are a lot of people gathering. I will be waiting.

The lanky paramedic waved a hand in front of her face. She shooed him off. "Would you please get your hand out of my face?" She walked around him and through the crowd of people who were taking snapshots of the odd trio.

The paramedics followed her out to her truck. One of the paramedics stepped in front of her. "I'm sorry ma'am. I must insist that you come with us."

She opened the door to her truck and sat behind the steering wheel. "Why?"

"If you go into a trance as you did back there, you could cause an accident."

"Again, I thank everyone for their concern, but I am perfectly fine. I was not in a trance. I was

27

ignoring you. Have a good day." She closed the door, started the truck and drove off.

~~~~~~

Another Realm…

He knew the king's weakness. In the form of a stocky, redheaded noblewoman, he opened a portal into a secluded area of the ballroom and stepped through unnoticed. He hated taking other forms, even human, but he didn't have time to wait until the king was alone. He needed to see him now.

This would be his last transformation, he swore. Each transformation cost him dearly, rendered him helpless for hours and sapped power he'd never regain. He frowned. If the king had been holding out, he'd withdraw the cost from his hide.

He gathered his royal blue velvet skirts, lifted them a few additional inches off the floor and weaved his way through the crowd in search of the king. Hundreds were invited to celebrate the tenth anniversary of the king's coronation.

"Long live the king," cheered numerous guests.

He went around the waltzers toward the cheers. The king was surrounded by several beautiful, slender women who fawned all over him. He maneuvered into the king's line of vision, acted shocked to see him, ordered his skin to blush, tilted his head in greeting, backed away, retreated to the opposite side of the ballroom and waited.

"May I have this dance," King Louis asked a short while later as he stepped from behind.

He batted his large green eyes at the king. "I'd love to, but," he lowered his gaze and his sweet, sultry feminine voice, "I'm afraid to dance in front of an audience."

King Louis held his hands out. "Then we shall dance in private." He led the way through the onlookers, up the castle stairs and into his private chamber. "I hope this is private enough."

He closed the heavy wood door.

"This should do nicely." He lifted the thick velvet skirt of his dress slightly and walked to the center of the spacious room. Large stones, tightly fitted together, formed the walls, ensuring no one would hear what transpired in the chamber. The only problem was the dim light. "Come here," he commanded in the female voice.

King Louis raised his brows. "My, this is a lovely surprise." He crossed over.

Switching from the soft, sultry voice of his female form to his own masculine, angry voice, he barked, "Where is she?"

King Louis gasped. "P-prophious? M-m-master." He bowed on one knee. "Forgive me, Master."

"Get up you imbecile. Where is she? I felt her presence." Prophious glanced at the kerosene lantern mounted on the wall. Its illumination increased tenfold and brought the chamber into full light.

The king stood, but continued looking at the floor. "She is not in this realm." He lifted his head. "I personally led the search for twenty years. You've rewarded me greatly. As king I have not stopped. Every inch of all four kingdoms has been searched."

"The elves must be hiding her in my realm. It's the only explanation." There were few places Prophious's powers couldn't reach. The elves domain was one of them. "It's a migration year for them," he said to himself.

"She's of the age to make her first migration."

"You have served me well. Return to your celebration." Prophious spun on his satin slippers, opened a portal with a wave of the hand and returned to his realm. He had arrangements to make before the debilitating effects of the transformation came to pass. All elves caught outside of their domain would be executed on the spot.

CHAPTER FOUR

Aurora's first stop was the army surplus store where she bought a duffle bag. At the bank she put her finances in order, so if she ever returned, money wouldn't be an issue. She also contacted her business partners and informed them she was going into retirement.

After hours of shopping for clothing more appropriate for Caiaphas, she only found one outfit and a few other items she thought might come in handy. Last, she traded in her sports utility truck for a used eighteen-foot bed, refrigeration truck.

You can t take those shoes. They don t even look right. Tahlan waddled through her walk-in-closet, over her shoes, boots and heels until he found a more appropriate pair. *These.* He tossed the leather sandals with his bill. *And these.* He kicked at a pair of boots.

She sat in the middle of the walk-in closet, surrounded by shoes. "I searched high and low for the perfect boots today and couldn't find them. My sneakers are the most comfortable shoes I own. Since I can't find the right thing, I might as well be comfortable."

But they don t fit in. And why are you packing so much? Everything we need is in Caiaphas.

"I'm going to wear the outfit I bought but," she began ticking off items with her fingers. "I'm taking a life's supply of underclothes, my backpack, towels, a small, but warm blanket, medicine, jewelry, several combs and as many sanitary supplies as I can squeeze in. You know. The essentials."

We have soap in Caiaphas.

"That's not all I meant by sanitary supplies. I'm ready. I just need to contact my therapist and cancel my appointment."

How does that phone thing work? He'd watched her using it when she made arrangements with her business partners.

She stuffed one of the pairs of boots into her duffle bag, then dragged the bag into her bedroom. "Wait a second, and I'll show you."

I wonder how much of our memories we'll recover when we return to Caiaphas. I already feel different. My memories of being human are returning. I have four brothers and a sister.

"That's great!" She sat on the edge of her bed and thumbed through her address book.

"We'll find both of our families when we return." She found Dr. Price's email address. "Okay. Let me give you the simplified version of how the phone works for most people." She sat at the computer, connected to her Internet email account, then grabbed the phone. "Someone speaks into the phone, and their voice is carried through this wire," she tapped on the phone cord, "to the person on the other end. The way you select where the wire will end is by the numbers you dial." She pointed to the keypad. "Each phone has a different number." She set the phone down on the TTY base.

Interesting. This world is full of amazing inventions.

At the computer terminal she typed,
Hello Dr. Price,

This is Aurora Church. I have an appointment for Thursday that I must cancel. I know this will sound crazy, but the goose I told you about was actually talking to me.

We went to the zoo today, and I met two others who are trapped in this realm.

Tonight I ll open the portal so we all can go home. I know you can t understand.

I m sorry about canceling at the last minute, but I don t have a choice. Have a good life doctor.

Peace.

She clicked send and turned off her system.

"Let's do this before he reads his email and tries to stop us. I'll meet you at the south fence of the zoo. You know, behind the aviary." She opened her bedroom balcony door. "I need to load the truck. I'll be there in about thirty-five minutes. Enjoy your flight, Tahlan."

I will.

~~~~~~

"This will be noisy. Keep lookout for me." Aurora watched Tahlan take to the air, then she lifted the back door of the truck and climbed onto the bed. She tripped over the eight-foot ladder, picked it up and set it on the ground, then felt on the bed of the truck for the gas-powered circular saw she'd purchased.

The dimmed lights from the zoo were barely enough to see the fence, let alone the inside of the

33

truck. *Why didn t I bring a flashlight?* She bumped into the saw. *Bingo.*

She knew there weren't any security guards, but she wasn't sure what other type of surveillance the zoo had. The buzz and grind of the saw reverberated loudly and interrupted the silence of the night. She quickly cut a gap into the chain-linked fence more than large enough for the truck to drive through. She pushed the ladder to the side, hopped into the truck with her saw and drove into the zoo. She laughed at herself. It probably would have been less noisy and definitely less time consuming to just drive through the fence.

"I'm in, Tahlan." She maneuvered the truck around the aviary onto the exhibit path.

So far no one has gone onto the road leading to the zoo. We re lucky there s only one road.

She backed the truck up to the alligator exhibit. "We're lucky there's nothing else out here."

Lamir waited at the gate. Aurora changed the saw blade, then cut the chains, opened the gate and ran to the back of the truck. She struggled to pull out the heavy ramp for Lamir to climb into the truck.

Someone just turned onto the zoo road, Aurora.

"Okay. He's almost in." She ran down to the raccoon. "Let's go." He didn't move. "I'm not playing. Get your big butt up and let's go." She hopped over the fence, wrapped her arms around the large fur-ball, then struggled to lift and carry him over the fence. "Well, you weigh as much as a horse," she teased.

Hurry, Aurora. They re almost to the zoo parking lot.

She ran back to the truck bed and heaved the overweight raccoon in. "I'm sorry, guys, but I forgot to bring a light. You'll have to be in the dark for a few minutes." She pushed the ramp into the truck, pulled down the door, ran to the driver's seat and gunned the engine to hightail it out.

The vibrations of the truck's engine shook her whole body. "Tahlan. I have to pass the person in the parking lot." She exited through the hole in the fence she'd cut and continued down the service path behind the zoo.

I'm on my way. You need to hurry I see the blue and red flashing lights you told me about. Head toward the forest preserve. I'll meet you there.

Aurora rounded the corner of the zoo into the parking lot. "I'm on my way." She saw Dr. Price in her headlights and brought the truck to a screeching halt. She rolled down her window and stuck out her head. "Move out of the way."

He held his hands up and yelled over the engine's rumble, "Listen to me, Aurora. I know you think the animals are speaking to you. But they aren't. Remember yesterday in my office. I told you to write a catalogue."

"Sorry, but I'm way past cataloguing, doc." She laughed. "Now please move out of the way. I'm taking us home."

He walked up to the truck and touched the hood. "This is your home. Come with me. I will help you."

"Tahlan," she yelled.

"He isn't real. I am real. I am here for you."

Tahlan swooped down and pecked and honked at the stunned doctor. Dr. Price swung at Tahlan, but missed the vast majority of his shots.

Aurora, go! I'll stall him until the flashing lights arrive. They'll think he's the one who broke into the zoo.

She slowly drove around the battling bird and doctor. Once they were in the clear, she pressed the pedal to the metal and made the great escape.

"Be careful, Tahlan." She turned onto the main street, then slowed her speed. "The cops... I mean flashing lights just passed me. They'll be to you in another minute or two. How is the doctor?"

I have him backed against the fence.

"Don't hurt him."

I won't.

~~~~~~

After meeting up at the south forest preserve entrance, Aurora drove as far as she could into the forest preserve, parked, then let her passengers out.

She set the oversized raccoon on Lamir's back. "When we cross over, I think someone needs to be put on a diet." She resituated her duffle bag, then followed Tahlan deeper into the woods.

She was shocked at how fast and easily Lamir moved over and through the brush. She had to keep her pace at a trot to keep up. "How did we get here, Lamir?"

I do not know. He climbed over a log. The raccoon dug his claws in to keep from falling off. *Get him off me. We are close enough for him to walk.*

She petted the scared creature. "He's terrified, Lamir." She set the raccoon on the ground and rubbed him behind his ears. "Don't be afraid, little one. Once we cross over, you'll be a strong, powerful war horse." She stroked his coarse fur a few times, then followed Tahlan and Lamir further into the woods.

"I feel a low vibration in the air," Aurora said.

That's the portal. Tahlan nodded toward the raccoon. *Look, he's starting to run. Even he feels it.* They all ran toward the vibration.

Trees surrounded them on every side, weeds and wild flowers were in abundance, but she didn't see any portal. "Where's it at?"

We can only feel its vibrations, Lamir answered. *The portal is not visible to the eye. Once you open it, the vibrations will be much more intense.*

She sat on the ground and unlaced her sneakers. "What's going to happen to us when we go through the portal?"

Lamir weaved his massive body between a few trees and settled down. *I do not know how long we have been away from our realm. I do not know how time works in this portal. The portals in our realm would only transfer you from one place in the realm to another. This is totally new to me.*

I hope the portal works in real time. I will go through first and protect the portal. Then Tahlan and the horse are to come through together. Last you, Aurora. Once we are all on the other side, we need to see how much time has passed. Tahlan, have you regained your memory?

I can remember everything except how I ended up here.

"Oh my goodness." She clapped. "That's great. I wish I remembered anything." She opened her duffle bag and took out her boots. What if we're put in different times or places once we cross?"

Then I want you to find the elves. Stay with them until I come for you. Tahlan will know what needs to be done.

Tahlan laughed. *So she's an elf. I should have known. Look at those ears.*

She ran her fingers over her rounded earlobe. "My ears are perfect, duck boy."

Perfectly elfin.

Lamir chuckled. *Okay you two. Listen up. We all have a bond that can never be broken.*

Aurora, our bond is fire. He motioned toward Tahlan. *We are bound by Aurora.* He focused on Aurora. *You and Tahlan have a bond that I cannot explain.*

"Can't or won't?" she asked.

Both. The portal entrance is part of this tree. Go ahead and open it.

She stood beside the tree. "How?"

Just wave at the tree and say open.

She shook her head. "That's entirely too easy. Don't I get some sort of magical words or something?" She swiped her hand toward the tree.

"Open." The air's vibration intensified, and the wind began to swirl. "Now that's more like it!" She dropped her head back and enjoyed the whirlwind. "Can we stay in here forever?"

I am crossing over. Put on your boots and meet us on the other side.

She lifted her gaze just in time to see the end of Lamir's tail vanish into the tree. "This is so neat." She put on one of her boots.

I'm not sure how long the portal will stay open, so don't take too long. I'll see you on the other side. Tahlan waddled next to the raccoon and urged him to step through the portal. A few seconds later, they disappeared into the tree.

"My turn." She scooted back to the duffle bag and put her arms through the straps. "It's now or never." She closed her eyes, inhaled deeply and soaked in all of the smells of the only home she knew, then stepped through the tree.

CHAPTER FIVE

Aurora, eyes closed, stood in the stillness of the night and enjoyed the clear sounds.

Chirping. She smiled with thoughts of crickets or some other insect. *Water running over rocks, maybe a river.* She shook her head. Sounded smaller. *Perhaps a creek or stream.* Slow, low, breathing. *Has to be Lamir.* She inhaled deeply. The air was crisp, clean and light with a hint of wild flowers.

"Before you open your eyes, I want you to remember I am a dragon," Lamir whispered.

She embraced herself and rocked. "This isn't a dream. I can hear." She wiped tears from her face and opened her eyes to see her world.

Her hands covered her mouth. A full moon hung low in the sky with its soft orange glow.

"It's beautiful." She stood between the edge of the woods and a small stream. Across the stream, fields of tall grass and wildflowers rolled for what seemed to be an eternity.

She looked from the fields to the woods on her other side. A few yards in front of her, a massive rock formation began where the woods ended. Around four stories high, the formation stretched along the curve of the stream until she could no longer see it. She glanced down and rubbed the goosebumps on her arm. "It's chilly here. I was always cold in the other realm. An inner cold. This is more intense. I feel it on the outside also."

Lamir spoke softly, as not to scare her. "You need my fire to stay warm until your body learns to produce its own. Come to me. I shall warm you."

She glanced over her shoulder at Lamir. "Oh my God," she gasped. He lay curled in the sand behind her.

"You have no need to fear me. Our bond is stronger than blood and can never be broken."

"I'm not afraid. I've just never seen anything so magnificent." She stepped to the side and back, then craned her neck to take in all of him. Her eyes traveled along his iridescent body as it gleamed in the moonlight in deep shades of red. She moved closer and stroked one of his golden claws that if straightened, would stand almost as high as she was tall. He lowered his head and revealed a ridge of sharp spikes that stretched from his nose to their omega at the tip of his spiked tail.

She hugged his muzzle. Her arms couldn't reach from nostril to nostril. "You are the most beautiful creature in any realm." She could feel heat seep throughout her body. A type of warm loving she'd only felt in dreams. "Who are you?"

"I am your oldest relative. I used to be human centuries ago."

"You're my dream father."

He chuckled. "I guess you could call me that."

"Thanks for not speaking. Sheesh, I'd actually be deaf now." She stepped away. "I didn't know humans could turn into other creatures. I mean besides geese," she jested. She scanned the area for Tahlan, thinking it silly to miss a goose. "So that's how you ended up with a human mother."

"I was once the most powerful sorcerer in the realm. I could transform into any creature I desired. I grew arrogant and cruel."

"This doesn't sound good."

"Power has a way of corrupting. Never allow power to go to your head, Aurora."

"Oh no." She shook her head. "I won't. I was adopted by a preacher and his wife. He eventually became pastor of what we call a mega-church. Obtaining power was all my parents cared about. They didn't make a move unless they thought it would be advantageous to them. It didn't matter how others were affected. What's your story?"

"I would transform into a dragon and destroy villages just to pass the time of day. I drew a sick kind of pleasure watching others suffer. I would cast spells that would spread plagues.
Start wars between tribes. I am ashamed of what I was. I am glad I was stopped."

"How?" She moved and snuggled into the bend of his leg. Unable to find comfort, she climbed up his neck and found the perfect spot between one of his head fins and a spike to settle into.

"Though I was the most powerful sorcerer, there was one even more powerful than me."

"God?"

"Humph." The vibrations from his chuckle rippled the waters of the stream. "I stand corrected. Two more powerful."

"Who's the other?"

"My wife. She slipped a potion into my dinner one night. If I transformed into another creature, I would remain that creature until I die. I am just grateful I did not decide to be a mouse."

She closed her eyes. "It's so great to actually hear someone speaking, the wind, the water, the bugs. In my dreams, I hadn't been paying attention to other sounds."

"My powers are limited. I could not give you full sound. I could reveal only what I had seen."

"So that's why you didn't have a face. Didn't you ever see your reflection in a mirror, or in the water?"

"To tell you the truth, I was showing you what I saw, your mind reworked my thoughts into the visions you saw."

"Why couldn't I hear in the other realm?"

"I do not know."

"I guess it doesn't matter. I can hear now. I could listen to Tahlan forever. His voice warms me." She rolled her eyes. "I'm sorry. I'm talking crazy. Back to you being human. What did you do to your wife?"

"Nothing. I loved her. I went into exile. While there, new laws were passed. Those who were of magic could no longer rule the realm."

"Why were we sent away? Who did it?"

"I can not remember. When I left, there was a battle for power. The king fell in love with and married a natural sorceress. Though he ruled, it was feared his children would be of magic."

"What's a natural sorceress?"

"Anyone can be trained in the ways of magic, but a natural sorceress is born with the magic in her. She does not need potions or spells. I was a natural. Most naturals are not nurtured properly, and their skills are not honed. By the time they are teens, they have lost most of their abilities."

"He changed the law so his children could rule, didn't he?" Her mind drifted to Tahlan, hoping he was safe. She shrugged it off. The majority of his memory had returned. He should be fine. She bit on her inner jaw.

"Yes he did, but he soon found that the queen could not bear children. Once the people of the realm found this out, there were power struggles. My memory has not fully returned yet."

"Simply amazing. Where's Tahlan?"

"Scouting the area. He says this is one of his hideouts. Traveling through the portal played with time. It was hours before he came over. The sun will be rising shortly, so I must leave." He pointed one of his powerful claws at the woods. "Go in about fifty paces, then turn left. Tahlan said there is a cave in the side of the rock plateau."

"How do you know we're related, and where is the rest of our family?"

"This is the last question I will answer, then I must leave. You were only two the first time you came to the zoo. Somehow you called to me. Only a relative could do that. You wanted to stay with me. I have been within you ever since. Teaching you through dreams."

Laughing, she slid down his neck. "I remember that temper tantrum. It's my first memory."

"Over the years, you kept coming back. I felt we had a special bond, deeper than family. Then when I made the bond complete with fire, I knew you were mine because you would have died otherwise."

She whacked him on the side. "Jerk. You could have killed me."

His loud rumble laugh shook the waters and trees and scared the forest creatures into frenzy. "No. I knew in my heart you were of me. It has been centuries. I do not know where the rest of our family is."

"How long will you be gone?"

"I am not sure. I do not know what has happened since I crossed over. I may be the last dragon. You go on into the cave and wait for Tahlan. Do as he says. He is the one your heart desires."

"He has a great personality, but I'm not into ducks," she grumbled. "Will I get cold again?" Thoughts of Tahlan's voice warmed her heart.

"You will crave the heat until your body learns to make its own. I do not want Prophious to know of my return, so you must stay with Tahlan unless you want to fly with me."

"Heck no. I'm not flying anywhere. I'll stick with duck boy."

"You will be uncomfortable until I can give you heat again, but you will live."

He stood on his hind legs, then glanced over his shoulder. "Back away to the tree line." He waited for her to move a safe distance away. "Once I am out of sight, you must hide in the cave and wait for Tahlan. He will keep you safe."

Whoosh, whoosh, flapped his wings, stirring winds and sand around him as he took off.

She grabbed onto a tree to brace herself until the winds subsided.

"You're beautiful." She stood in awe and watched him glide across the sky into the darkness.

Go to the cave, Aurora.

She walked onto the beach and retrieved her duffle bag. "I'm on my way. How far does this telepathy stuff work?"

I can barely hear you, but I feel you.

"Well, I hear you loud and clear." She walked to the base of the stone plateau. It felt smooth and cool under her hands. "If it's this cold in the cave, I may need you to come back sooner than later for a little heat."

She pushed the brush and branches out of her way and trudged through the woods in search of the cave. A hundred and fifty paces deep, she turned and retraced her steps. Still no cave. "This is stupid."

I can feel your frustration, Aurora.

The sound of Lamir's voice sent her heart in a panicked race. "Stop doing that... Dang. You scared the buggeebies out of me."

I can not hear you, he interrupted. *You need to find shelter in the cave. Feel along the wall of the rock. The cave is above your head.*

"Oh great. Now he tells me," she grumbled and traveled along the wall, this time looking up. The trees blocked most of the moonlight, but sixty steps in and six feet up hung the entrance of the cave.

She took off her duffle bag, pushed it over her head along the wall and into the cave. She stepped back and bumped into a tree. The tree's branches were too weak to climb, and she couldn't see well enough to find anything to stand on.

She stood against the wall and stretched as high as she could. Her hands only a few inches away from her destination, she stood on her tiptoes and strained to reach the lip of the cave to pull her bag back down to stand on.

Her body warmed, especially around her waist, and she slowly rose. She didn't care how Lamir worked his magic but was glad he did. Once high enough, she gripped the ledge and pulled herself up, then dragged her duffle fully into the cave.

The sound of someone scrambling into the cave set her senses on high alert. She leaned flush against the wall and prayed to blend into the darkness.

An imposing figured stood before her and radiated a heat she longed to absorb. Silent, she held her breath and hoped the figure didn't really know she was there. It was too dark. There was no way he could see her.

He gently caressed her jawbone down along her neck and shattered her hopes. Instead of fear engulfing her, his heat comforted her, warmed her soul. "Who are you?" she whispered breathlessly. Unable to resist his heat, she rested her head on his chest. He embraced her, surrounding her with glorious heat. Their hearts synchronized. "Thank you," she paused, "Tahlan."

His low chuckle confirmed his identity. "How is my favorite elf?" The feel of her smile on his chest somehow warmed his own heart.

"I'm not an elf." She walked to the edge of the cave into the morning light that broke through the trees.

He stepped out of the darkness. "Have you looked at your ears lately?"

"Oh my," she gasped. "It's you," she choked on her words. "This can't be." The warrior she'd created for the game. Her heart's desire.

Her eyes traveled slowly along his body, starting with his sandaled feet, along his battle-scarred bare legs, powerful thighs. She gulped and continued her journey over the ragged edge of his leather kilt and breechclout.

She subconsciously licked her lips, wanting to taste the bitter sweet of his dark chocolate chest, shoulders and neck. She'd always loved a man in locs, and his were long and partially pulled back into a ponytail with the rest falling over his shoulders and down his back. His stern and handsomely deep facial features were better than anything she'd drawn. She fanned herself.

He needs to cover himself.

He held her around the waist and pulled her into his firm body. "You like what you see?" He bent and suckled her neck.

She dropped her head back. "You're practically naked. How else could I react?"

He gazed into her face. Lamir had said she would fulfill all of his desires. *How did I miss those soft auburn eyes, perfectly sculpted nose and succulent lips?* He knew what he desired at this moment. He slipped his fingers into her thick hair and massaged her scalp. She moaned her pleasure.

"You react as you should." He swooped her up and carried her fully into the cave.

"Put me down, you silly goose." She laughed and wrapped her arms around his neck.

The dawn light crept into the cave. He could clearly see his pallet neatly folded along the wall. He kicked the bedroll free, then gently set her on it.

"Why thank you, kind sir." Completely exhausted, sleep couldn't come too soon. She pulled off her boots and socks, then set them to the side. He took off his sash and began taking off his kilt.

"Whoa big fella. Sheesh." She turned away and shook her head. "Some men have no shame," she mumbled.

Speaking of shame, she covered herself with the rough blanket and took off her clothes, leaving only her bra and panties on. Before, when Tahlan had seen her nude, he'd been a goose. This was totally different.

She folded her clothes to use as a pillow, then lay down with her back to whatever Tahlan was doing. She could hear him scramble around. She wanted to sneak a peek, but didn't. She snuggled under the scratchy wool blanket, waited for sleep to overtake her and prayed for more inner heat.

"It's too hot for blankets." He removed the cover and cupped her into his body. She was about to slap him for uncovering her, but somehow his touch increased her inner heat.

He reached around and brushed her lips with a tiny piece of root. "You need to eat this."

She swallowed the bland root, then cuddled against his bare chest and absorbed the heat he freely gave. The feel of him slowly grinding his hardness against her rear caused her to stiffen. "Wait a second."

His hand slipped along her flat stomach. "I've waited long enough," he grumbled.

She crawled away and scrambled for the blanket. "Sorry," she covered herself, "but I don't do that. I didn't mean to mislead you. I thought you were giving me heat." She realized his nudity and threw the blanket to him. "Cover yourself. Dang," she drawled out. "What's wrong with you?" She turned away.

He knelt behind her and massaged her neck. "Why are you acting like this? You want me as much as I want you. Don't worry. The contra root will keep you from getting pregnant."

He kissed her neck. She batted him away. "I'm not playing, Tahlan. I don't have sex."

His mouth dropped open in horror. "What?"

CHAPTER SIX

"Turn around and look at me, Aurora. What's this nonsense about not having sex? Everyone has sex."

"I don't want to see you naked, and everyone doesn't have sex. Not where I'm from." She hugged her legs with hopes of holding in some of the heat. When he stalked away in anger, he took his heat with him.

"I'm wearing a tunic. Now turn around, and let's discuss this like adults."

She peeked over her shoulder and saw him sitting a few feet away wearing a dark tunic with his legs crossed. She turned her body toward him, but kept her eyes to the ground. "I didn't mean to make you angry. I was raised in a Christian church and taught that sex outside of a loving committed relationship is a sin."

He softened. "I'm not angry with you. I'm angry at the Christian church for teaching you that crazy nonsense." He scooted closer and took her hands into his. "Sex is for pleasure. By the time a person is thirteen, they have usually started having sex. It's not as great as flying, but is the next best thing."

He placed her hands on his powerful chest, gave her heat and warmed her soul. "I'm a warrior. One of my only pleasures in life is sex." *And giving you heat.*

She withdrew her hands. "But don't you believe in love? Don't you ever want to marry? Have children? I want to save myself for the man I love and who loves me."

He traced the sad lines of her face with his fingertip, wanting to wipe them away. "Trust me on this one, my little elf. You do not need to save sex. You will not run out."

Her lines of sadness transformed into a sheepish grin. "I'm not an elf. What about falling in love?"

"I can't afford to fall in love. If my enemies found out, they'd use my love against me. I'm a warrior and must live as one."

Her eyes blinked quickly to bat away the tears. The one her heart, body, and soul desired refused to love her in return. "I understand." Freezing, she crawled to the pallet and wrapped herself with the scratchy wool blanket. "I am not a warrior, so will wait for love." Eyes closed, she prayed for warmth and sleep.

Not sure how to proceed, he sat quietly and watched her tremble. As soon as he crossed over from the other realm, he knew something was wrong. He was human again, but he wasn't quite himself. His memories of Aurora weren't his usual lust-filled memories of women who crossed his path. They were of the laughter and arguments they had shared. He wanted to create more of those memories. He drew his fingers through his long locs. For the first time in his life, he was scared.

His heart, body and soul all ached for her. But he was a warrior, and his enemies would hurt her if he allowed himself to fall in love with her. That was the one pain he knew he couldn't bear.

He lay behind her on the pallet without touching her. "I will give you the heat you need." He slipped his hand under the cover and slowly pulled her toward his body.

She inched forward. "I don't know how this happened, but I love you and won't mislead you. I'm not having sex with anyone who doesn't love me. Lamir said the cold would be uncomfortable, but won't kill me."

He chuckled. "You must be the most stubborn elf ever." He held her still, then leaned against her body. "I'm keeping you warm because you are cold, not because I want sex. I'm holding you because it brings us both pleasure." Giving her heat also cooled the fires within him—the fires that raged since he lifted her into the cave. He couldn't explain it, but he more than wanted to touch her, he also needed to touch her.

Under his caressing touch, she relaxed slightly. "Do you like the way I make you feel?" he whispered over her ear.

"Yes," she murmured. He rolled her onto her back and kissed her waist. "I don't want to lead you wrong. We should stop," she said.

He gave her nose a little peck. "You are very straightforward. You couldn't mislead me if you wanted to. I'm only doing what you allow. Bringing each other pleasure is not a sin, Aurora. Once you see how this realm works, you'll change your mind about sex. Then I'll bring you the greatest pleasure you will ever feel."

She noticed he didn't mention her saying she loved him. She wouldn't push the issue. With time, he would see she was correct. "But won't all of this teasing wear down on you."

He gazed into her eyes. "You're worried about me?" Only women paid to pleasure ever cared, and they were more interested in the money. "You're special to me." He turned her into his body and held her close. "Sleep without concern, my little elf. With you I give and receive pleasure." She relaxed. "When we're in town, I shall take pleasure from other women until you're ready to share my bed fully."

She twisted away. "What?"

He sat up. "Surely, you don't expect me to stop having sex?"

"How can you use women like that?"

"It's their job. They make good money. This is a different realm, Aurora. You aren't being fair. I can't return your love, but I am willing to give you pleasure. You are the only woman I will give pleasure. That is as far as I can go."

Her mind spun out of control. "You've got to be kidding!" The realities of this realm were overwhelming. She said a silent prayer for patience.

"Try to see it from my side. How would you feel if I slept with other men?"

"After refusing me, I'd be extremely angry and kill them, so don't even think about trying it," he warned. "This is different. I'm not refusing you. I'm not even replacing you. These women are nothing more than a release. I won't give them pleasure. I only give you pleasure and you give me pleasure."

She slowly lowered her head. "You just don't understand what I'm saying," she whispered. "Sex is not sex for me." She peered into his dark eyes and searched for understanding. "It is a physical way of expressing love. In the other realm, some call it making love. I'm not mad. You do what you have to do."

Her sorrow stirred unfamiliar feelings within him. He actually felt guilty for wanting sex. He shrugged it off. Once she saw the realities of the realm, she'd understand and come to him.

He held his hand out to her. "We need to rest. Come to me. I will give you heat." She hesitated, then snuggled in, but he could feel the emotional barrier she'd built. "Give it time, Aurora. You will see that I'm correct."

He couldn't stand the barrier she'd thrown up, but he couldn't give her what they both wanted. "You are special to me. Do you think I'd lie like this with another woman? Do you believe I speak with others the way I've spoken with you?" He felt her shields weakening. "Do you think I trust anyone the way I trust you? You gave me your complete trust and friendship when you thought I was a goose. What we have is special. I don't want to lose it. I'm giving you all I have to give."

She grinned, rolled over and wrapped his arms around her.

"What's so funny?" he asked.

"You love me, but won't admit it." She yawned. "I love you, too."

"I'm not in love with you, Aurora."

"Be quiet, duck boy. I need my rest."

He watched as the rise and fall of her breaths became shallow, and she eventually fell asleep. "You are one hardheaded elf." He kissed her cheek.

~~~~~~

Tahlan felt Aurora move. He pulled her close. "Where do you think you're going?"

"I'm hungry." She removed his arm from around her waist. "I need food."

He stretched. "I'll catch some fish. Do you know how to make a fire?" He searched through his tools for his fishing spear.

"Sure. Matches plus dry wood equals fire." She winked, then poured the contents of her duffle bag onto the cave floor and began sorting. "I'm taking over this wall by the way." She grabbed her toothbrush, soap, razor, deodorant, matches and clean underclothes, then wrapped them all in a large bathing towel. "Where should I build the fire?"

"What are you doing with all of that stuff?"

"I'm taking a bath in the stream."

"You took a shower yesterday. Build the fire. I'll be back in a few minutes with lunch."

She went to the edge of the cave and leaned over. "How the heck do I get down?"

"Did you hear me? We don't have time." He pointed to the clear blue sky. "It's high noon. I want to reach town before nightfall." He needed to get away. Sleeping next to her was hard enough, but now... He sighed. Her curvaceous body and the contrast between her red satin underthings and her caramel skin had him running on high.

She created a pouch for her supplies in the towel and tied it in a knot. "I heard you. I'm just not heeding. I'm not a warrior. I bathe daily." She dropped her supplies to the ground. "Now help me down."

He brushed her ribcage with his hands. A heated charge rushed through her. "For people so uptight about sex, you all sure don't dress the part." He pulled her into his hard body and ground gently. "I remember women on the sand wearing these." He flicked the back of her bra. "What's wrong with men from that other realm?"

She turned in his arms and rested on his chest. "Your heartbeat is so strong. I've heard so many different, beautiful sounds."

"You think my heartbeat is beautiful." He chuckled. "Now that's a new one."

"It is. And so is your laugh. It rumbles."

"I could hold you all day long. But we have work to do." He released her and leapt off the ledge. "Jump." He held his arms out, and she jumped without hesitation. He caught her and helped her with the landing.

"When we go into town, you can't dress like this in the open." He ran a finger along her waist. "This is for the bedroom, not outdoors."

She spun slowly with her arms to the sides. "You like what you see?"

"You're playing with fire, little elf girl."

"Umm, you know how I love the heat." She grabbed her supplies and made her way through the brush to the stream.

"For a virgin, you're awfully brazen."

CHAPTER SEVEN

"The water's great. Come in with me." Aurora stood on the streambed, bent slightly so her ears would be water level, closed her eyes and listened to the water flow by.

Tahlan waited at the shore with his fishing spear and watched Aurora, instead of catching their lunch. He still couldn't believe he hadn't noticed women the whole time he was in the other realm. "I'm busy." Memories of seeing women dressed in the tiny outfits, like Aurora was wearing, flooded his mind. *How do men in that other realm resist all of the temptation?*

"I'd be willing to bet there are more fish in here than out there."

He ignored Aurora and walked along the tree-lined portion of the shore in search of a school of fish while keeping a watchful eye on Aurora.

She swam down to his location. "Wouldn't it be cool if there were such things as fish whistles or even a fish call?"

"A fish whistle? You're being ridiculous."

"And you're too serious. Now work with me here. Close your eyes." She closed her eyes, flung her arms in the air and called, "Up fish!"

To Tahlan's amazement, hundreds of fish leapt out of the stream. The splashes of the fish landing startled Aurora.

"What was that?" She ran out of the water to Tahlan and wrapped her arms around him. "Something's in the water."

Still stunned, he could only say, "Fish. Lots and lots of fish. You're safe."

Before he could explain, she pushed him into the water. "How could you say fish? Piranha are fish, and I don't want to be in the stream with them." She jumped in, then climbed onto his back. "Now you'd better stop throwing rocks in the stream. You could have actually scared me."

He glanced over his shoulder into her amber eyes. She had no idea what she'd done. Just as when he'd seen her reaching for the ledge of the cave. She'd hovered several inches off the ground when he helped her finish her ascent.

She wasn't an elf for sure, but how could she do these things? He decided to keep her in the dark for a while longer. Once in town, he'd find someone to help figure out her true identity and the source of her powers.

"Are you paying attention to me?" she asked.

"No."

Feigning disappointment, she dropped off his back. "You said no. Oh my. Now you're gonna get it." She dove under the water and pulled one of his legs from under him.

He went under, but grabbed her foot before she escaped. He pulled her into his arms, rose out of the water and threw her.

"Wheeee…" She flew thirty feet downstream. She swam back to him with the enthusiasm of a child on Christmas morning. "Throw me again."

He knew he was strong, but not that strong. He kept his peace and threw her again. They spent the afternoon jumping from trees into the stream, playing chase, catching fish and having an all-around great time.

"I'm starving." Dressed in an oversized tunic, she walked out to the lip of the cave and sat beside Tahlan. She noticed the heat from the fire didn't warm her, but being close to him did. Confused, she knew she'd figure out the heat thing someday.

He handed her a plate of fish. "We'll leave for Garland first thing in the morning. We've lost a day."

"You had a ball." She carefully picked at her fish for bones. "There's no telling what we'll come up against. It's a good thing we turned loose now." She tasted the fish. "This is delicious."

He had to agree with her. He couldn't remember the last time he'd had fun as a human. He watched her devour the fish. He'd forgotten what it felt like to live life and enjoy being alive.

Aurora made life more than duty. She made life worth living. He stopped his thoughts. He couldn't allow himself to fall in love.

"After we check out Garland, if all is right in the world, what will you do?" she asked.

"This is my father's province. Depending on how long I've been gone, my oldest brother may be its ruler now. Either way, I will run one of the sectors."

"So you'll hang up your warrior skirt?"

"I was wearing my dress uniform yesterday, not battle gear."

"I was only joking, duck boy. Don't get your panties in a bunch. Will you settle down?"

"If I found the right elf." He winked and took part of her fish. "Do you have any memories?" He couldn't believe talking about marriage didn't revolt him.

"No. None yet. Do men rule here?" Besides language and showing her a few creatures of the realm, the Lamir-induced dreams didn't teach her much.

"Yes. But women are very valuable because they are outnumbered at least four or five to one. For a man to get a wife," he shrugged, "well you get the picture. A woman can have her pick of any man."

"So what's a good mate in a woman's eye?"

"He has to be able to produce her lots of sons. I have four brothers and one sister. A man that is an only son and has three sisters will have difficulty finding a wife. He'd need to have a lot of property and power if he'll have any shot at finding a wife."

"Why would they want sons so badly?"

"It's a vicious cycle. Because there aren't enough human women to go around, it's a dangerous world for women. No one messes with women from strong male families. So women want sons and brother-in-laws to help protect them."

"They don't want daughters at all?"

"Most women want at least one daughter. I've known women who have five or six sons before having a daughter; then she stops having children.

Needless to say, the female of the family is usually spoiled. I also know men who lie about how many brothers they have."

Her eardrums suddenly felt like they would explode. She held her hands over them. "Ouch! Dang, why does he do this?" She gritted her teeth.

Tahlan stood and grabbed his battle-ax. "What's wrong?"

"It's Lamir. He's so loud... Prophious is still alive and has taken over the whole realm. He has appointed a wizard ruler in each province." She shook her head. "He's saying something about the military waiting for your return. Whew." She sighed. "Thank God he broke the link. I need to teach him volume control."

He gazed into her eyes with a sense of loss. "I'll die a warrior, Aurora. Tomorrow we go into Garland. I want to see for myself how the realm has changed. Prophious was a cruel sorcerer of the likes I'd never seen before. He must have killed the king and queen." He caressed her face. "I don't know how you fit into this, but I'll protect you from Prophious."

"I'm not afraid of him."

"That's my brave little elf." He stroked her perfectly rounded ears. "Did you bring a comb? I want to adorn your hair with my ribbons so everyone will know you're a part of my clan." She scrunched up her face. "Remember, I told you about women with strong male families. Our family crest is on the ribbons of my dress uniform. Or would you rather have my musty, old leather headband and sash?"

"I'll take the ribbons. And I'm not an elf."

They cleaned the dishes in the stream, then she sat between his legs while he meticulously brushed and combed out her long, thick, black hair. She'd fixed her hair in one thick braid after her shower, but playing in the steam had kinked it up again. Unlike her adoptive-mother, Tahlan didn't seem to mind combing her hair at all.

"You need to have locs or braids if you want to keep your hair so long." He smoothed her bushy hair back into a ponytail with a leather strap. "You could never fight with hair like this. You'd get all tangled in it," he teased.

"Do the people here come in different colors like in the other realm?"

"Yes. I guess we're the same, just in a different place." He carefully combed out her hair. "When we're in town, I'll buy you more clothes." A few hours and long conversation later, he had weaved in the ribbons as he braided her hair into one long braid. "All done." He dropped the braid onto her back.

"I did something wrong. You can barely see the ribbons, and they aren't showing the family crest. We'll also have a headband engraved with the family crest made for you."

She felt the braid. "It's tight. I like it. What other women's hair have you been doing?"

"Only my sister. I told you women are spoiled."

"Well keep on spoiling me. I like it. How will we get to town?"

"Night, my warhorse."

Her mouth dropped wide open. "You mean that fat raccoon is actually a horse? I thought Lamir was joking."

"More than a horse. He's the finest warhorse ever. He's hidden nearby." He rolled out their pallet. "Now come to bed. This may be our last night of peaceful sleep for a while."

She snuggled in and absorbed the heat he freely gave. "I think I'm addicted to your heat."

The heat came from within and without.

He nibbled along the brim of her ear. "Goodnight, my little elf."

"I'm not an elf," she murmured groggily. In her mind, his braiding her hair confirmed he loved her. She knew that in no time he'd forget his silly, warriors-can't-fall-in-love business and admit his true feelings.

CHAPTER EIGHT

Prophious woke, but he held onto his dream. Visions of a fire orb loomed before him.

Within the orb he saw dragons destroying his armies and—he squinted—flying fish. The effects of the transformation hadn't fully worn off, but he could sense her presence.

What does it mean? There hadn't been a dragon sighting in over forty years. Dragons and elves didn't mix, so dragons wouldn't hide in the elves kingdom. She was somehow part of the dragon. Maybe someday she could transform into a dragon like the mighty Lamir. A chill went down his spine. Lamir was dead. He had to be. All dragons were.

Flying fish? He smoothed his hand over his silver mustache. She must have discovered his powers couldn't touch many of the waterways or her sign was water. Either way, she'd stay close to the water.

A fire orb. He drew in a deep breath, then released it slowly. The orb put him in mind of the house of fire's family crest. *The visions are contained within the orb.* He smiled. *She's in the fire province.*

He waved his hand and the vision disappeared. He always knew oracles were overrated.

~~~~~~

"Are you sure he's a horse and not a black giraffe in tacky leather armor?" Aurora stood five eight, and the horse's back was taller than her. "Does he bite?"

Tahlan rubbed Night's muzzle. "He's gentle." He took her hand and allowed the horse to smell her. "He won't hurt you. I think he may even remember you from the other realm."

Night nudged Aurora under the neck. "I think you're right. He just gave me a horsy kiss."

Tahlan mounted.

She continued petting Night. "How far away is Garland?" She walked around to the side of the horse and held her arms up.

"Only three hours." Tahlan lifted her onto the horse and placed her in front of him. "I'll buy you a horse in Garland." They rode off at a canter.

"How many horses did you see traveling down the road in the other realm? I don't know how to ride."

"In this realm, you must know how to ride. I shall teach you." Slowing down to a trot, he guided Night through the woods. "Never come into the woods alone. Prophious's element is earth. He can use his powers to control many of the plants. He's also mastered controlling animals. Birds are his favorite. He can see what they see."

"That sucks. So why is a bird's element earth instead of air?"

"Birds are air, but Prophious's powers are…" he trailed off. "I can not find the words to explain. In order to control an element not of your own... We are up against a formidable foe."

Aurora took in the view. The trees looked the same as trees in the other realm. If she didn't know better, she would have sworn she was in one of the national parks, but the crisp fresh air was a dead giveaway. She inhaled deeply.

He caressed her face. "Are you tired? We'll be through the woods in a bit and can take a break." She'd been quiet for such a long time, he wondered what she was thinking.

She closed her eyes, momentarily, and rubbed her face into his caring palm. "I'm not tired." She leaned her back against his chest. "I was just enjoying the air and sounds. I'll bet one breath of air in this realm is equal to about five in the other realm. And the animals sound like a symphony."

"What's a symphony?"

"A giant band of different instruments playing together in harmony. Sounds here aren't distorted like in the other realm. I love the sound." She could see the field he'd told her about through the trees.

"When we're around people, keep your talking to a minimum. You use words no one has heard of."

They exited the woods and sped up to a gallop. Night stepped through the tall grass with no problems.

"I'll try to remember."

"See the mountains to the left. They're the end of my father's province. Since Prophious has taken over and replaced the rulers with his wizards, I must find my family. My parents may be in the mountains." He paused. "I don't know how my mother and sister would survive without our castle."

"You're a prince? Ooo, la, la, I'm sitting with royalty."

"I'm not a prince, you silly elf." He kissed her ear. "I'm a warrior. My family used to rule this province. When I was young, wars broke out between the elves, sorcerers, humans, and everyone else who wanted to rule the realm. Everyone wanted to dominate the others."

He slowed Night. "By the time I was sixteen, the humans were losing more battles than winning. The price of losing was death or enslavement. I couldn't bear the thought of my mother and sister becoming slaves or dying. Like many men, I became a soldier."

"Did you know Lamir was king centuries ago? He's the reason the no one of magic could rule law was made."

He sped Night up. "I'm not surprised. I've never seen a dragon as powerful as him. Place your hands on mine. It's time for you to learn to ride."

She followed his instructions.

"Close your eyes and feel the rhythm. Every horse has his own stride. Don't fight it, move with it. Become one working unit." He increased Night's speed.

"He's so graceful, Tahlan. I almost feel as if we're running on air."

Night began rising off the ground. Eventually, they were riding above the tall grass.

Aurora couldn't hear Night's hooves hitting the ground or legs brushing through the grass. She opened her eyes. "This is so cool. Why didn't you tell me horses in this realm literally walk on air?"

"Close your eyes, and we'll lower to the ground. Feel it with Night."

She followed his instructions, and they were on the ground again.

"That was great. When can we do it again?"

"Not all horses can fly. We must make sure we're out of sight when we do it. In town, we shall pretend you're half-elf. Most people haven't spoken to an elf before."

"Good thinking." She stroked Night's neck. "You're the greatest horse ever."

An hour later, she pointed to a dark spot that littered the horizon. "What's that?"

"The guard tower outside of Garland."

As they approached the stone tower, two guards ran out and stood at attention.

"Commander. I'm sorry. We weren't expecting you. I shall alert the captain immediately."

"At ease," Tahlan ordered. The guards relaxed slightly. "I'm not here on business. I'm here for pleasure." He splayed his hand across Aurora's waist and held her close. "If anyone finds out I am in town,

I'll hold you personally responsible. Do you understand me?"

"Yes sir, Commander, sir." The guards nodded.

"I'm leaving my gear in the base of the tower." He dismounted. "You may return to your post." The two soldiers bowed, then ran back to their post.

"What do you command?" Aurora whispered.

He led Night to the back of the tower, then helped Aurora down. "A commander is the military leader of a province. There are only seven of us. I was the commander of the neighboring province on the other side of the mountains and my oldest brother was commander of this province."

"Well how did they know? I don't see any rank on you."

"Night's armor for one thing." He opened a cellar at the base of the tower. "And once we were closer, this." He took off his sash and handed it to her. "Only commanders have these crescent marks. I shouldn't have worn it." He put all of his and Night's gear into the cellar along with her duffle bag. "Now we can continue."

She watched him mount Night. He held his hand down to her. "Let's go," he ordered. She stood with her hands crossed over her chest. "What?" he asked.

"I think you look better in a dress. You look like an upright log. When we're in town, I think you should add more color to your wardrobe."

His cotton shirt and trousers were dark brown. His boots were black. "Get up here, you silly elf." He pulled her onto the horse, and they continued their journey. "This is not a military outfit. I wish to blend in with the other men."

"You, blend in?" She laughed. "You're a giant who rides a giant horse and carries a giant battle-ax. How can you blend in? I say you wear the dress."

"And what if I needed to fight? Could you imagine the spectacle of seeing men fighting in dress uniform?" He chuckled. "Now that would be funny."

She glanced over her shoulder into his dark eyes. "Are you actually joking with me? Who are you, and don't bring back the other Tahlan." She kissed his chin, then looked forward.

He frowned. He was joking, wasn't he? Keeping his emotional guard up around Aurora was virtually impossible. He pointed at the town. "It's grown so much."

"I can't tell large distances very well. I'm guessing about four laps around the track. Yeah, that's at least a mile across. I wonder how deep it goes. Boy, I feel like I'm riding back into time. Maybe jolly ol' England with a magic twist."

"Aurora."

She ran her hands over his forearms. "I love it when you say my name. I think you're a baritone. Say it again."

"You are talking about things I've never heard of. Must I kiss you to keep you quiet?"

"Sounds good to me."

"Are you sure you're a virgin?"

"I'm a virgin, not naïve, and not a baby."

There were quite a few people on the streets as they entered town. He stopped Night and scanned the area. The two to three-story wood buildings that lined the streets put Aurora in mind of an old west town.

"The livery should be somewhere close." His feelings of unease increased. What he saw didn't match what he knew. At least, what he thought he knew.

"What's wrong, Tahlan?"

"These people don't belong here," he whispered. "Remember what I told you about women being outnumbered?"

She saw his point immediately. "Almost everyone is a couple. They look like they're here on vacation or something. Look at the shopping baskets."

A couple walked by, nodded a hello and continued.

"Their clothing is also out of sorts. Most women can't afford such fine costumes. Hats, gloves. What material are those dresses? Velvet, silk? And what is wrong with their hair? It should be down or in braids. Why is it all bunched up like that?" He spotted the livery and pointed Night in the correct direction.

"Maybe Garland's changed into a honeymooners' paradise. You thought we were only gone two years, but maybe it's been longer." She played with her thick braid. "Hair fashions do change with time. These people look like they come straight up out of Regency England times to me. And the businesses remind me of the wild, wild west." Her nose scrunched up. "I smell the stable."

They entered the livery. Tahlan dismounted and helped Aurora down.

"May I help you, sir?" The proprietor stepped out of his office and into the barn. He wiped his filthy hands on a dirty rag, then held his hand out.

Tahlan shook the heavyset man's hand. "I'll be boarding my horse for a few days and wish to purchase a second horse. I'm looking for a good riding horse and saddle."

"I might need to charge you double for him. He's a big one," the man joked. He took the reins and led Tahlan's horse to a stall. "What's his name?"

"Night. I'll feed and groom him myself."

"That's what I expected. I received a new shipment of horses this morning. You may wish to pick one out before the soldiers come in tonight." He closed the stall and escorted them to the barnyard.

"Stay here." Tahlan released Aurora's hand, then jumped the fence to examine the horses closely.

She climbed onto the bottom rung of the wooden fence. "You have a beautiful selection of horses."

The proprietor leaned against the fence. "Thank you. I've never seen a horse the size of Night before. He's an incredible beast."

"Tahlan," she called. "I want a pretty one." He rolled his eyes and continued inspecting the horses. "You won't be in trouble for selling to us first, will you?" He looked at her crossways. "Is something wrong? I wouldn't want to cause you trouble."

"Yes, I'd be in trouble," he finally said, "but your man will give me twice what the military will pay. This isn't the first deal I have made like this. You're just the first person to care if I would be in trouble."

"Well don't worry." She smiled. "We won't tell anyone. By the way, my name is Aurora. Pleased to meet you." She bowed her head.

"I'm Thomas, and the pleasure is all mine." He tipped his head with a slight smile.

He had an acceptable voice, but nowhere near as deep and rich as Tahlan's or Lamir's.

She guessed him to be a tenor. "Do they have chronicles in this area? Something that tells the events in the area?" she asked.

His eyes lit up with understanding. "You mean the newspaper. It comes out once a month. I save them in my office."

"Can we have one of your older ones? We'll pay for it."

He nodded toward Tahlan. "Looks like he's found you a horse. The newspaper is yours for free." He turned toward Tahlan. "You picked a beauty."

Tahlan stood before the two. "Someone ordered a pretty horse. Come over here, Aurora."

She climbed the fence and went to his side.

"What do you think?" he asked.

"I think he has the longest eyelashes I've ever seen. I love him." She rubbed his muzzle.

"He is a he, isn't he?"

"No. He's a she." Tahlan loved being the source of her pleasure. "I'll take her. Keep her in the stall next to Night."

"Yes, sir. Now someone needs a saddle."

"That would be me." She climbed over the fence. "Does she have a name, Thomas?"

Her back was to Tahlan, so she missed his face; but Thomas didn't. Tahlan's black eyes burned through Thomas. "You may name her," Thomas uttered. "I'll draw up the paperwork for you." He hurried off.

"What got into him?" she asked. Tahlan hopped over the fence, and she hugged him.

"Thanks for Sable. She's beautiful."

"Sable?"

"The mare you just bought me." She looped her arm around Tahlan's and followed him into the stable. "Thomas has a newspaper for us."

"Was he bothering you?"

"No. I was bothering him, so you'd better be nice."

He grumbled and entered the office. "While I handle the business, get your backpack out of the saddle bag. Then we'll be off."

She left the men alone.

Refusing to look up, Thomas pushed the newspaper across the table. "I meant no disrespect. She gave me her name, so I thought you were her brother…"

"Stop," Tahlan interrupted. "She spoke to you first?"

"Yes, sir."

"She doesn't know our customs. She is mine. I should have explained to her not to introduce herself to men. There is no harm done." He took out his money pouch.

"You two make a handsome couple. I'm sure you'll be happy together and have many sons. The horse is five pieces of gold. Two doors down, at the leather shop, they sell high quality saddles for two to four pieces of silver. She'll like them." He began writing out the receipt. "Do you want me to brand the horse for you? No extra charge."

"Put a white tattoo on her right hind quarter. The same mark I have on Night." He placed the coins on the desk. "How much is the boarding fee?"

"Two bits a day."

"I'm all ready." Aurora entered the office and stood beside Tahlan. "I can't believe you bought me a horse. I can't wait to ride her."

Thomas put the money away in the strong box under his desk. "You two enjoy your stay." He handed Tahlan the newspaper.

"Is Garland a tourist town?" Aurora asked.

Thomas gazed into Tahlan's eyes for permission to answer. Tahlan nodded.

"Yes it is," Thomas answered. "The others leave before sundown."

"Others?" she asked.

"The tourists. The town is ours again from dusk till dawn."

"Where do these tourist come from, and where do they go from dusk to dawn?" Tahlan asked.

Thomas shrugged. "Prophious won't tell us. They come daily, purchase our goods and leave."

"Thank you for everything." Tahlan escorted Aurora out. "I don't like this."

"You worry too much. These people are here spending money in Garland's shops. They can't even stay long enough to mess up the city. That's a good thing. I wish we had this in the other realm."

"But where do they come from?" He saw the leather shop Thomas had told him about.

"I don't know, but as long as they aren't hurting anyone, who cares? I know you grew up in times of

78

war, but things have obviously changed. What's the date on the paper?"

He'd forgotten about the paper. He unfolded it and began reading. "This can't be correct."

She glanced over his arm and scrunched her face. "It's written in jibberish. What does it say?"

His gaze locked on hers. "According to this, I've been gone for thirty-four years. This... this is impossible."

She hugged him. "After thirty-four years of a *normal* life, a few days ago a goose convinced me to jump through a portal to a different realm. Believe me when I say, I understand impossible."

He tipped her face up and grinned. "Are you ever serious, you silly elf?"

"We have to play with the hand we're dealt. My life was lonely growing up. I couldn't dwell on negatives. I had to make the best of every situation."

"You're right. But something still feels out of place. I'll hold my judgment." He stopped in front of the leather shop.

"After we buy a saddle, can we go shopping for clothes?" she asked.

"What's wrong with what you have on?"

"Look at me." She held out her arms. "Brown boots, cream leggings and an ugly green tunic. I look like a jacked-up elf. You told me to buy this getup."

"Well," he laughed, "that's what you get for listening to a goose. Do you realize I took a shower with you and had no sexual desire for you whatsoever?" He pulled her into his body and suckled along her neck. Heat raced through both of their bodies. "Now, that's impossible."

CHAPTER NINE

"Tahlan, come back here. I look like a purple genie." She watched herself in the full-length mirror. "Eat your heart out, Barbara Eden."

Tahlan peeked around the partition at Aurora. His manhood went to full attention. "You can't wear a dance costume on the streets." He stepped fully behind the partition and pulled her close to his body. "I love this," he whispered. "I'll buy it for you, but you can only wear it for me." He nodded toward the dresses she'd hung on the partition ledge. "Pick one of the velvet or silk dresses for the street. You should blend in with the other women."

She glared at the pile of underclothes she'd tossed to the side. "I can't wear all of those layers of clothes. I'm not used to it and don't even know how to put them on. I saw a woman wearing one of these outfits. Why can't I?" She leaned her head on his chest and absorbed the heat while she listened to the strong, steady beat of his heart. Soon he'd realize the fighting in the realm had ended, and they could live happily ever after.

"She was a dancer. You are not."

She turned in the narrow space and folded her leggings and tunic. "All I'm saying is I can dress as a dancer and be comfortable instead of in these hoity-toity layers and layers of clothes."

She handed him her old clothes, then sorted through the things she wanted to buy. "And I have new riding clothes. I'd rather wear them than those stupid dresses."

"I know the women in the other realm dress in even less, but the men here are different. You need to cover yourself up. And have you seen any women roaming the streets in riding clothes? You need to blend in."

"But I'm with you. No one will bother me. There's no way you can blend in. Plus, look at this." She pulled out a large purple chiffon scarf from beneath the underclothes. "I had a feeling you'd have a conniption fit, so I found something to cover myself with. I even have the matching veil. All anyone will see are my eyes, perfectly rounded *non-elf* ears and sandaled feet."

He frowned. *Conniption?* "You're to stay close to me and not speak to any males."

She brought her hands together, as if in prayer, and bowed. "Yes master. Your wish is my command. What's our next stop?"

"While you were trying on half of the city, I spoke to a few people. Just about everyone I knew has moved on, and there is no word of my family. The proprietor of the magic shop is one of my closest friends. You'll enjoy his shop."

"Since he'll be an old man, can I speak to him?"

He raised a brow. "If he's blind."

~~~~~~

Tahlan scrutinized the confused elderly eyes of his best friend.

Somian tilted his balding grey head. "Tahlan?"

82

I've really been gone thirty-four years. Tahlan glanced over his shoulder at thirty-four-year-old Aurora. She winked; he rolled his eyes and turned toward Somian for answers. "You have aged well old friend," Tahlan rumbled.

A broad smile spread across the old man's face. "I'd know that voice anywhere. You've finally returned." Somian motioned his frail hands for Tahlan to come closer. "Come close so these old eyes can see you."

Tahlan walked around the piles of books that littered the floor and stood in front of his friend. "You were always a powerful man, Tahlan, but you really look alive." Somian peered up into his face as if reading the answer to the meaning of life. The wrinkles in Somian's face seemed to smile with his grin. "Prophious will be defeated." He peeked around Tahlan and saw Aurora standing quietly in the doorway. "Don't be afraid of me." He held his hand out to her. "I don't bite."

"Tahlan, may I speak?" she asked with a coy smile tipping her lips.

"Somian, this is Aurora."

She crossed the cluttered room and shook Somian's hand. Instead of releasing his hold, he held tight. She felt a recognition of forces, but she didn't understand it.

"You are from this realm, but you are not from this realm," he murmured. His cold green eyes locked on her amber eyes. She could feel him searching, but it didn't scare her. She knew Tahlan wouldn't allow anyone to harm her.

After a few seconds, he released her. "You must help Tahlan put an end to Prophious's rule so the realm will be free again."

"From what I've seen thus far, there isn't anything wrong with the realm."

"I know, little one." He patted her hand. "Your eyes will be opened tomorrow."

"I want to know today. Tahlan, what's he talking about?"

"I don't know." He took her by the hand. "We need a few questions answered, Somian. Where is my family, and can you tell us who Aurora is?"

"Aurora is the dawn of a new day, and your family is still in this province. You two must work together to bring Prophious's rule to an end."

"You won't tell us anything else, will you?" Aurora grumbled.

"I want to give you something." Somian went behind the counter and searched through the dusty shelves. "Here it is." He handed her an old leather bound book.

She blew off the dust and examined the book closely. "This is very kind of you, but I can't read." She set the large book on the counter, opened it, and then lightly brushed over a few pages with her fingertips. The aged paper was coarse to the touch. The worn, ink-filled pages somehow emitted a slight heat.

"Keep it. It is a gift from our last queen."

Wide-eyed, she pushed the book toward him. "Oh no. I can't. It's too valuable. If I lost it, I'd feel lower than dirt. Please take it back."

"She gave it to me, but it was never mine."

"Tahlan, help me here."

"Somian is an oracle. He sees things we don't. Take the book."

She sighed and handed the book to Tahlan to put in her backpack. "I'll take excellent care of it." She bowed slightly. "Thank you, Somian."

"You're welcome. What do you think of the shop, Aurora?"

Several locked trunks occupied one corner. Built-in shelving units with vases, wands, jars and items she didn't recognize took over the walls. "There's a lot of interesting stuff to get into. Is it all actually magic?"

"Yes it is. While you are here, I shall show you how they work." He tossed a knowing smile at Tahlan, then returned his gaze to Aurora. "All will be revealed in a few days. I wish I could give you more."

"You'll have to start teaching her tomorrow. It's getting late, and we need to check into the inn."

Somian nodded. "Then I shall see you tomorrow."

~~~~~~

The sights and sounds of the pub kept Aurora's attention. "I can't believe these places actually exist. When will the show begin?" She turned away from the stage, took off her veil and set it on one of the extra chairs at their four-chair table, then cut a leg off the baked chicken and put it on her plate. "This smells delicious."

"I don't know if they have a show tonight." Tahlan slopped a few mashed potatoes onto her plate, then set the platter in front of himself. "Barmaid," he called. "I need a jug of ale and bottle of milk."

"Who's drinking milk?" Aurora looked around the room for other women besides the help. She found none.

"You." He dipped a few heaping spoonfuls of peas onto her plate.

"Wanna bet?" An unfamiliar musical plucking caught her ear. She looked over her shoulder and saw someone playing a lute. "Oh cool, they are having a show. But why is he sitting off stage? Oh, there's a second guy."

"Eat your meal before it gets cold." He continued eating. "The show is for men. Not women. You'll enjoy the music, though."

Two dancers sidestepped onto stage to the rhythmic thump of one of the musicians flat handing his lute. The audience hooted as the ladies began their dance.

"Oh my goodness. You'd think they never saw a woman before," Aurora said.

"The dancers have a choice of any man in here, just as the barmaids do. Before marriage, women make a good living."

She glanced at Tahlan who seemed to be hypnotized by the sway of the women's hips.

"You are so rude. How can you stare at those women with me sitting right here?"

He began eating the chicken breast. "Aurora, you're more beautiful than those women, but I'm a man with needs. You've kept me on hard for days now. I need a release. One of them will be my release. We've already discussed this."

"But, Tahlan."

"But what?" he snapped. He continued watching the dancers. He could tell the taller one with the long red hair was attracted to him. He smiled and nodded a hello.

"But nothing. Do whatever you want." She pushed her plate away. The barmaid placed their drinks on the table. "Thank you, ma'am."

He looked into Aurora's pouting face. "You have no need to be jealous. Caiaphas is not like the other realm. If you want me, I am here for you. I'm not rushing you. I can wait, but it isn't fair for you to expect me to do without sex." He poured her a glass of milk. "You barely ate. Drink this. You'll like it." The music died down, and the dancers left the stage.

She drank the cold, sweet milk. "Oh, now this is good milk."

He smiled. "I knew you'd understand. I need to speak with the young lady. I'll keep my eye on you. Do not talk to anyone." He pushed away from the table.

"I'm jealous, Tahlan. Leave me alone to drink my milk."

"You're mad because you aren't getting your way, not jealous. You're just as spoiled as the rest of the women in this realm. It's only sex."

She narrowed her gaze on him. "Why are you talking to me?"

The dancer approached Tahlan. He took her by the hand and led her to the bar where they sat and chatted.

"What a jerk." She picked at a few peas. For some reason, all sound was drowned out by the dancer's giggles. Aurora had no idea what Tahlan could have said that was so funny. She poured a second glass of milk.

She noticed all the men were watching her every move, except the man she wanted. She choked when she saw Tahlan kiss the dancer on the mouth. He hadn't even kissed her on the mouth. She slammed her glass of milk on the table and turned away.

The dancer's high squeal grated on Aurora's nerve. She needed to concentrate on something, anything else. She tuned out Tahlan's tart the best she could and listened. The musicians could barely be heard over the noise of the crowd. She closed her eyes and concentrated on the music. The *pluck, thunk, thunk* of the lute brought forth memories.

Though her hearing was distorted in the other realm, she could always feel the beat and loved to dance.

This beat reminded her of an Egyptian belly dance she'd seen on television. She imagined this was what it sounded like. She swayed to the beat with thoughts of all she'd missed when she couldn't hear properly.

She thought about the dancers' performance. These men didn't know anything about dancing, and the women knew the men were desperate. All the women did was sway their hips and hold their arms out. She wasn't mad at the women. After all, according to the standards of the realm, they were earning an honest living.

She watched Tahlan pull the dancer onto his lap; he had the audacity to tell her to blend in, then made a spectacle of himself in the middle of a bar with a woman. She wondered what happened to all of this so-called danger they were in. He didn't seem worried to her.

She finished off her milk. Since they'd arrived, the most dangerous thing she'd come across was body odor. She fanned her nose. People in this realm obviously couldn't bathe regularly.

"She's the most beautiful woman in the world, but beauty isn't what I need right now." She heard Tahlan say to the dancer.

Aurora felt her face flush with embarrassment. How could he put all of her business out in the street like this? She looked from the stage to the musicians to Tahlan. *What's good for the goose is good for the gander.* She grabbed her scarf and crossed over to the musicians. "Will you play for me? I wish to dance. I'll give you three bits each."

"We'll do it for free."

She tilted her head in thanks. "Start out slow please. I need to warm up." She looked over her shoulder. Tahlan hadn't even noticed she'd moved. "You'll know when to increase the pace." She shook out her chiffon scarf, then placed it over her head and shoulders like a hooded cape, leaving the rest to drape to the floor. She stepped out of her sandals and nodded to the musicians.

As requested, they started playing their lutes slow. With each graceful step further onto the stage, she slightly opened the scarf more, as if she were a butterfly opening its wings for the first time. The men took notice of this quiet, yet potent, entrance. They turned to watch what would happen next.

Wings fully expanded, she bowed forward. The men began to clap and approach the stage. She grinned, thinking they hadn't seen anything yet. As she rose to the gradually increasing beat, she brought her arms forward and up until they met above her head. This caused her whole body to be cocooned within the scarf. She stood still and waited for the mistrals while she listened for Tahlan.

Tahlan missed her entrance, but the applause of the men brought him to full alert. "What is she up to?" he grumbled. The music's pace increased. She slipped one leg out of the purple shell and traced several small rhythmic circles on the floor with her big toe, then withdrew the leg. "She wouldn't," whispered Tahlan under his breath.

The men begged for more and pushed each other for a closer view.

"What's wrong?" asked the dancer. "Don't you want me?"

"Oh no." Tahlan's heart raced and inner heat rose. He couldn't rip his eyes from Aurora.

The dancer caressed his chest. "Let's go upstairs. I have a room."

"I can't right now." He pushed the dancer away. "Wait a minute."

Now finished teasing the audience with one leg at a time, Aurora began to twist her body.

From the tips of her fingers, the twist worked its way down to her feet. She heard Tahlan telling her to stop, but she didn't. Instead, she continued the twist as she slowly brought down the scarf and exposed her whole body.

Tahlan weaved his way through the crowd and commanded her to stop. Several men tried to keep him from advancing, but he was too strong.

She continued her erotic butterfly dance until Tahlan ripped the lutes from the musicians.

"The show is over," he barked. "Aurora, come here!"

She bowed and waited for the applause to die down, then calmly exited the stage and gathered her sandals as she descended the stairs. "Thank you very much," she said to the musicians. "Tahlan, would you please pay these gentlemen five bits each?" She thought each man had earned a two bit tip.

Too angry to speak, he stood still.

"We won't accept payment. We thank you." They escaped quickly.

She could practically hear the vein in Tahlan's forehead pounding. "You don't look so good, Tahlan. I hope you didn't catch anything from your dancer." She sauntered across the pub with her head held high and hips swinging and retrieved her veil from the table.

Before Tahlan could regain his composure, men began asking for time with Aurora. They offered astronomical sums of money. He wanted to kill each of them for daring to look at Aurora. But this was her doing. She'd done this on purpose because she was angry. And angry for what? She refused to have sex with him, not the other way around?

Aurora approached him. "I'm tired, Tahlan. Can we go to our room?"

"I should give you to one of these men."

She raised a brow. "I'm not yours to give. Did you enjoy my dance? I thought it might help you get in the mood."

CHAPTER TEN

Aurora stripped for bed, but left on her matching purple satin bra and panties. "Are you planning on staring at me all night? Say something, turn around, or get out. I'm sleepy." She sat on the edge of the small, lumpy bed.

"Why are you so hardheaded? Didn't I tell you about men in this realm?" Tahlan barked.

She blinked several times. "This room is only what? About fifteen by fifteen. I now hear perfectly. You don't have to yell. And didn't I tell you I was jealous of that woman? Why would you disrespect me like that? Couldn't you wait until I was out of sight or at least out of earshot?" She threw a bean filled pillow at his head.

She found it hard to speak over the lump in her throat. "Why would you flaunt her in my face like that? Why were you trying to humiliate me?" She sniffed and wiped the tears from her eyes. "How did you feel when those men called for me? I saw your face. You were jealous. Now, how would you have felt if I'd have kissed and groped them while you watched? If I had insulted your manhood?"

She buried herself under the scratchy, wool blanket and turned her back to him. "You can stand there looking stupid all night for all I care. Just blow out the lantern."

All the fight blew out of him. He'd never been jealous in his life, especially over a woman. Their purpose was to give men pleasure. When she performed for those men, he had become enraged.

She was his. He didn't want to share any part of her. He wanted her for more than pleasure. He looked at her curled up under the cover, shivering.

She was right when she said he'd flaunted. He wanted to make Aurora accept he was a man and had needs. Hurting her wasn't his intent, but the result. From now on, he would be careful and hide his sexual activity.

He changed into his tunic, blew out the lantern and crawled into bed with her. She scooted forward. He pulled her close. "Don't start that. You need heat. All the blankets in the realm will not warm you. Only I can." He brushed a few stray hairs behind her ear. "Your dance was like none I've ever seen," he whispered. "You are the one for me." He kissed her ear. "You are the only one I want." He caressed her waist until she relaxed and eventually fell asleep.

Memories of her erotic dance flooded his mind. He wanted to make love with her so badly he hurt. He dressed quickly and crept out of the room.

~~~~~~

Tahlan waited for Sherri, the redheaded dancer, to undress. He relived every move of Aurora's dance in his mind and became hard. He held Sherri down to the bed and kept his promise to Aurora, not to give pleasure. He pumped into Sherri while thinking of Aurora until he had his release.

He washed himself, then dressed. "How much do I owe you?"

"Ten bits."

~~~~~~

Tahlan felt like a new man as he crept into the room. He should be able to go a few days without sex before the urge grew strong again. His keen ears picked up the sound of Aurora weeping. "There's no need to be scared. I'm back to warm you." He took off his shoes and trousers, then crawled into bed with her.

She batted, kicked and screamed at him. "Get away from me! Get away!"

He backed off. "Aurora, it's Tahlan. Wake up."

"I am awake you… you… Ewwww… Just get away from me."

He heard more than saw her scramble across the small, musty room to a corner. He stooped beside her. "What's wrong? Did you have a bad dream?" He held out his hand. She'd told him of the nightmares she had as a child of strange gorilla sized, monkey-like creatures chasing her. "Come to bed with me. I'll protect you. You're cold. I will give you heat."

She pushed his hand away. "What part of get away from me don't you understand?"

"What in the realm is wrong with you? Why are you angry at me this time?"

"Why am I angry? Are you out of your mind or do you think I'm stupid. First you flaunt your whore in front of me, but that wasn't good enough for you, was it? No you had to…"

"It's not like I brought her in here. Damn. You were asleep."

"I was asleep until you called to me to dance for you." Her words slapped him with the force of a typhoon. "I thought it was a dream, until I changed into that redheaded dancer. I heard and saw everything all the way to you paying her ten bits. You know we have a telepathic link I don't know how to control. You used it to hurt me."

"Aurora, I didn't mean to." He reached for her.

"Don't touch me." She leapt up and went back to the bed. "You disgust me."

He knelt beside the bed. "I swear. I would never." Her tears tore at his heart. "I was only using her as a release. I snuck out thinking you would never know. I'm sorry." He could feel her shutting him out. He wouldn't allow it. He needed her.

He dropped his head. "I didn't know. I would never hurt you like that." He lifted his eyes and locked them on hers. "I made a mistake earlier this evening. I've learned from it. I really didn't know."

The moonlight barely provided enough light for her to search his eyes for the truth. He sounded sincere. She lowered her lids and turned away, acknowledging the ways of the realm. He knew no other way. "It better not happen again, Tahlan. I may forgive, but I'm not God. I don't forget." She returned to bed.

He lay in bed beside her. "I swear to be more careful in the future. You are the only one I want. You."

She relaxed slightly and prayed for sleep and to forget the events of the night. In time, he would see they were meant to be. She sighed, hoping he'd figure it out sooner than later. Being understanding became more difficult with each breath.

He tried to cuddle, but she shrugged him off. He waited until she fell into a deep sleep, then pulled her close. "I'm sorry. Someday you will understand this realm is different."

~~~~~~

Governor Chanterelle inhaled several calming breaths, bowed before the smokes of the incense and cast a spell of vision. His master had been acting out of sorts lately, and the news he had wouldn't put a smile on his face.

The smoke twisted and twirled until it weaved into Prophious's likeness. "Master, I have good news for you. We have located their hiding place."

"Why have you called me through smoke?" With a slight wave of his hand, Prophious's smoky image transformed into full living color.

Chanterelle bowed and scraped as he backed away. "Smoke is the fastest." He slowly rose, but kept his head down. He couldn't look Prophious in the eyes and tell him he'd failed.

"I am in no mood for games." Prophious extended his arm and constricted his hand.

Chanterelle could feel Prophious strangling the life out of him.

"Now will you tell me what I wish to know, or would you like to continue playing childish games?" He released his grip, and Chanterelle dropped to the floor.

Chanterelle took a few seconds to catch his breath. "Forgive me." He stood and looked into Prophious's lifeless, black stare. "I have failed you, but I will not again."

Prophious raised a grayed brow. "So you did not catch them?"

"I have not. But my apprentices were able to find their hideout," he added quickly. "We know they are in Garland." He stood silently and watched the most powerful person in the realm. Fearing, yet admiring him.

A man of average weight and height, the eighty-year-old Prophious looked like an everyday, run of the mill, middle-aged, balding man. The heavy burgundy master sorcerer cloaks he wore made him look more grandfatherly than fierce. He held a quiet, potent power that left others wondering what he was capable of.

Chanterelle recalled the myth of another sorcerer whose quiet presence and powers exceeded Prophious's. Unlike Prophious, there were no safe havens from Lamir's reach, not even the elves' kingdom. He knew the stories of Lamir were just fairytales told to apprentices to give them something to strive for. Lamir was the ultimate. He glanced at his master. Prophious would be the closest any sorcerer could come to being the ultimate.

"I must know where they are," Prophious snapped.

Lately Prophious had been on edge. If he didn't know better, he'd think his master was scared. "Master, I know this is not my place. But why are you so concerned about an elf?"

Prophious frowned. "Summon Oracle Delanda."

"She died ten, maybe twelve, years ago." He held out his hands. "Master, if I may be so bold."

Prophious nodded. "Speak."

"The magic anomaly you sensed may be a small band of elves. This is the year of their migration. And I have sent for dragon slayers…"

Prophious lurched forward. "What dragon? You mentioned nothing about dragons."

His gaze dropped to the floor. "Master, please allow me to explain. There have been no dragon sightings for over forty years. I have never seen one in my lifetime. There were tracks that I think may be dragon. I wanted to make sure before I told you."

"Are you sure Oracle Delanda is dead?"

"Yes, Master." He lifted his gaze. "Shall I call for Oracle Somian?"

"No. Unlike you, I am not sure where his allegiances lie. The realm is in danger, and I will need your assistance to save it."

Chanterelle stood tall and proud. "I would die for you, Master."

"Dying won't be necessary at this time." He flashed a quick grin. "But your obedience will be. Are you familiar with the legend of Lamir, the sorcerer who was once king?"

"Of course, Master. It was my favorite fairytale growing up."

"It isn't a fairytale, and he didn't go into self-imposed exile." He waited for Chanterelle to regain his composure. "Over four hundred years ago, Lamir was the greatest sorcerer that ever was or will be. His reign was brought to an end by his wife. He loved her deeply, but she was very jealous of the people's love for him."

Chanterelle's eyes popped wide open. "Lamir was real?"

"Yes. I can transform into animals, but nowhere near as well as Lamir could. He could be an ant one second and a dragon the next. One day his wife poisoned his food, and when he transformed, he could not return to human form. He now lives his life out as a dragon."

"You think the dragon tracks were Lamir's?"

"Yes. There is more. Lamir is no longer on the side of magic. He remained neutral until I began my struggle for power fifty years ago. He destroyed the first army I'd amassed, but then he disappeared. I thought he'd been killed. After I became ruler, Oracle Delanda told me a prophecy that I forbade her from repeating."

He stepped closer to Prophious's image. "Did she tell you Lamir would return and destroy the realm?"

"There are several parts. In short, she said Lamir's return would bring the dawn of a new day, and the daughter born of fire magic would take her rightful place on the throne."

A spark of understanding lit Chanterelle's eyes. "So that's why all females born of magic are put to death."

"Yes. That is also why I eliminated the king and queen before she bore any children. There are no rightful heirs. Do you know of the warrior Tahlan?"

"Everyone does. He was the greatest warrior ever and the commander of Surien. He died in battle, didn't he?"

Prophious slowly explained, "No one knows. Oracle Delanda believed he was sent to find the child and raise her as his own. I think Lamir hid them for all of these years and has now returned. Tahlan will be an old man by now, but the child... With Lamir as her magic mentor and Tahlan as her fight instructor."

The hairs on Chanterelle's neck stood on end. "I understand, Master. I will have the military surround the town."

"No." Prophious held out his hand. "We must not involve the military. The majority of them are awaiting Tahlan's return. They believe it is the sign for their revolt to begin. This must be a war of magic against magic. Before Oracle Maki died, he told me to keep this prophecy from materializing I must separate the child from Tahlan. She draws her strength from him. Find her and bring her to me, immediately. She is young and impressionable. I will make her my queen and fulfill the prophecy."

Chanterelle nodded his head. "Yes, Master. What about Tahlan?"

"He is of no use to me. Once I have the girl, no one   can   touch   me."

CHAPTER ELEVEN

"I have finished drawing your bath, sir," whispered the orderly. "And placed the oils beside the tub as you requested." He quickly skimmed Aurora's body with his eyes, then looked down. "She is beautiful, sir. You are very lucky."

Tahlan caressed her waist and kissed her ear. "Did you see her show last night?" He would be the envy of every man in the province. Everyone would know she belonged to him and him only.

"I'm afraid I missed it." He set two towels on the end of the bed. "Her performance is the talk of the town. You should be proud."

"I am. Take three bits off the table."

"Thank you." He took the generous tip. "Enjoy your stay in Garland." He stopped in the doorway. "If you need anything, ask for me, Jerol." He left the two alone.

"Aurora," Tahlan whispered. "I have something for you."

"I'm tired." She turned into him and snuggled. "I don't want anything but sleep."

"I happen to know you'll want this more than sleep. Hold onto my neck." He lifted her as he rose, then slowly lowered her into the lavender scented waters of the tub.

"A hot bath." She smiled. "A real live hot bath. How did you do this?"

"I think you called it room service." He poured a dab of oil onto his palm, rubbed his hands together to heat the oil, then massaged it into her shoulders.

She tied her braid in a bun, then allowed her head to fall forward. "This is glorious. What have I done to deserve such treatment?"

"I love bringing you pleasure. You're the only one I will ever bring pleasure." He handed her the lavender bar of soap, then continued massaging her.

"Is everything about pleasure for you?" She glanced over her shoulder into his deep eyes. "What about love?"

"Love isn't for everyone. I am either fighting or seeking pleasure. Before meeting you, the vast majority of my time was spent fighting. I've seen too much death and destruction. I have to take pleasure when I can because I don't know when I'll have another chance."

"How can you kill people?"

"I'm not proud of the blood on my hands." He stroked along her jawbone with his knuckle. "I don't have a choice. I must be hard or many more will die. I must sacrifice myself for the greater good."

"I understand. You keep us all safe." Blinking repeatedly, she turned away, lathered the soap and smoothed it on her legs. "What is on our agenda today?"

"After we feed the horses, I need to scout the area. You can spend the day with Somian. He's hiding something from us."

"Can we trust him?"

"Yes. He's an oracle and withholding because we aren't supposed to know yet. If he gives too much information, it'll harm us, not help."

"I'll look around town also. I may be able to find something out. Where's my razor?"

"No, Aurora." He searched through her backpack, then handed her the razor. "You stay with Somian until I come for you."

She smiled, admiring his dark, handsome face. "I don't know why you say these crazy things to me when you know I'm gonna do my own thing. I'll meet you back here tonight for dinner. Now why don't you leave so I can finish my bath?"

He raised his hands. "I'll be places I can't take a female, so you'll get no argument from me this time."

"Excellent."

"But you must follow my rules." He ticked them off with his fingers. "Do not introduce yourself to men. You will dress in your riding clothes or in a walking dress. Stop talking about the other realm. If you haven't seen it in this realm, do not mention it."

He frowned. "Absolutely no dancing. You're free to roam the streets in the morning, but you must spend the afternoon with Somian. Meet me here at sundown, not a second later."

She laughed. "I can't remember all of that. I'll try to be a good girl. It gets dark awfully early, and I may need more time with Somian. How about we meet at his shop?"

"Then we shall meet at Somian's, my little elf. Do not be out late."

~~~~~~

Aurora continued watching the interactions between the visitors and the inhabitants of the town. Though cordial to each other, she sensed an underlying fear on both parts.

She also found it odd that the townsfolk didn't shop during the day. They all worked in the shops until the visitors left. From what she'd seen, Tahlan had been correct about the female shortage. It just wasn't as drastic as he portrayed.

A whiff of fresh baked bread caught the attention of Aurora's growling stomach. She slightly lifted the skirt of her walking dress and followed the wonderful aroma and the sounds of people chatting to the outdoor farmers market.

"Would you like to buy a basket, Miss?" asked the merchant whose booth lay just outside of the corded off market.

Everyone who shopped in town carried wicker baskets. "May I have a small one please and two of the cloths?"

He placed the cotton napkins in the bottom of the basket, then handed it to her. "No charge."

"Oh, but I can't." She dug through her pouch for a few bits. "Please take this."

His lips tipped up at the corners. "I can't take your money. How could I charge you after the performance you gave last night?"

A young couple stood patiently and waited for him to serve them. "I'll be with you shortly," he told the couple, then focused his dark brown eyes on Aurora. "You travel alone today."

She stepped to the side. "Take care of your business. I'm not going anywhere."

After he assisted his customers, he turned his attentions to Aurora. "Your dress is lovely."

"Why thank you." She spun in her pale yellow walking dress. "I hate dresses, but I thought this one was nice. Tomorrow it's back to riding pants."

He drew his head back in surprise. "Why would you wear pants? You're too beautiful to wear pants."

"Why thank you, again." She flushed. "People are so kind here."

His eyes twinkled with mischief. "People or men?"

She laughed. "You sound like my significant other. All he does is hound me about how men think."

His tone became serious. "Aren't you ready for marriage?" He stood and gave her his stool to sit on.

"Of course I am."

"I have a hundred and sixty-three gold pieces and four pieces of silver. If you want to marry, half goes to your family. We can work here during the day and make beautiful music together all night."

She lowered her gaze to her lap. "I'm sorry. I didn't mean to mislead you."

"I have two brothers and no sisters. I would like at least one daughter, though."

"That's not it. You see, I'm marrying Tahlan."

"That soldier?" He drew his cream-colored fingers through his dark, shoulder length hair.

The realm had definite male-female roles she had issues with, but at least the people didn't care about race.

"Why you women always want his type, I'll never know. He's a warrior. They don't marry. You're waiting for something that will never happen."

"I don't know why I'm telling you this, but he says the same thing. I just feel that he's the one for me."

"Don't you want children? Your soldier will not change. If the prophecy is to come to pass, he will be leaving soon."

Excited, she leaned forward. "What prophecy?"

"No one knows the whole prophecy, but in the thirty-fifth year of Prophious's rule, the military will be led to victory when the chosen one returns. This is the thirty-fifth year. Soon we will be free, but your Tahlan will most likely die in the battle. Prophious's magic army is very strong." He cupped her face in his hands. "Do not fall for soldiers. We need them to protect us. We're grateful, but they do not marry. Especially his type."

"I've kept you too long." Heart heavy, she sighed. "It was nice speaking with you."

"You know I speak the truth. You're still young enough to have children. If you wait on him, you will regret your decision."

She couldn't listen any longer. He was just as wrong as Tahlan. "I'll see you around."

"Dorian. My name is Dorian. And what is the name of the lady of my dreams?" He held his hand over his heart and winked.

"You are silly. My name is Aurora."

"I hope to see you tonight." He kissed her knuckles. "If you allow me, I can bring you great pleasure."

She stepped away. *Is sex the only thing the men in this realm think about?* "I'm flattered, but I must pass."

Aurora made her way through the market. She stopped in front of the bread stand and inhaled deeply. "May I have two slices of bread with light butter and a loaf for later?"

The vendor opened the wooden bin and handed her a loaf of bread, then turned to prepare a warm slice for her. A little boy sneaking between the produce booths caught her eye. She hadn't seen any children since she left the other realm. The sight of this mousy-haired, filthy boy was a shock and welcome relief.

She almost choked when he stole an apple and placed it into his back pocket. "May I please have two additional loaves of bread and a jug of milk?" The vendor handed her the additional items. She paid him.

"Hey, come back here," yelled an angry, heavyset man. He grabbed the little boy by the collar and dragged him around the counter. "I'll have you horsewhipped." He patted the squirming little boy down and found the apple.

"Excuse me, sir." Aurora caught the outraged man's attention. "What has my baby brother done? Come here Remmy." She snapped her finger at the boy and pointed for him to stand beside her, but the child didn't move.

The man's eyes traveled from the scraggly, little, white boy to the very well-kept black Aurora. He raised a brow. "This," he paused, "is your brother? I doubt it. I'm turning him over to the authorities."

"Yes he is. We have different fathers." She took out her coin purse and handed the man a silver piece. "This should cover anything his sticky fingers have touched. Come here, Remmy," she ordered.

Without hesitation, the little boy took her hand and followed her out. "My name is Aurora, what is yours?"

"Nerrin."

Once outside the farmers market, she set down the basket and took out one of the cloths she'd bought. "Where are your parents?"

"My mom been gone long time. My dad at work. You nice." He grinned. "You marry my dad and take care of me and my brother."

Her heart went out to the little boy. She wiped off his hands and handed him a slice of bread. He stuffed the whole slice into his mouth.

"How old are you?" she asked.

He spit out half of his bread with his answer. "Seven. Can I have some for my brother?"

"Stop eating so fast. There is more." She handed him the jug of milk. "Drink it slowly so you don't choke. After we finish shopping, I want you to take me to your father."

His eyes opened wide. "You marrying my dad?"

"No, darling." She brushed his disheveled hair into place with her fingers. "I'm marrying someone else. I still want to meet your family." She wiped his mouth with the second cloth, then took him by the hand and headed for the boutique.

He pulled her away from the door. "I can't go in there. I'm not allowed."

She looked at a few of the visitors. They were staring at Nerrin as if he had a contagious, fatal disease. *So women and children have the lower positions on the totem pole.* "We're going inside this store and buying you some new clothes and boots."

Somian was correct, the real danger in the realm had just been revealed to her. She opened the door and pushed Nerrin inside. If this was going to be her new home, it was time to start changing it for the better.

Nerrin tried to hide behind Aurora's legs, but the clerk trained her eyes on him. "Is this little ruffian following you, Miss Aurora. I'll call my husband immediately."

"No he isn't. Thank you for your assistance. I need trousers, shirts, and boots in his size." She pulled him around and made him stand in front of her.

The clerk looked down her long nose and watched him shift his weight from foot to foot. "You aren't serious are you? Miss Aurora, please," she whispered, "we don't serve his kind here. What will my customers think?"

"If you do not get the clothes immediately, I will cause the scene of all scenes. What do you think your customers will think about that? And did the leather shop deliver my headband down here?" She began looking through the denim pants. "Here you go, Nerrin. I think these will fit. Try to find some that will fit your brother."

His eyes traveled from the outraged clerk to Aurora. He stopped slouching and helped Aurora pick out the clothes.

"After this, we'll go to the market and pick up a few groceries."

"Groceries?" he asked.

"Food supplies, darling."

CHAPTER TWELVE

Nerrin burst into the hut. "Jon, guess what I found."

Without looking up from his sewing, Jon snapped, "Where have you been? The field master sent that flunky Korliss to tell me you weren't there. We've been deducted two bits." He glanced up from his work and saw Nerrin. He frowned. "Where did you get those clothes? What's going on?"

Nerrin set a large basket of food on the table. "Wait 'til you see what I brung home. She's pretty, rich and my sister." Beaming with pride, he brushed off his chest. "We adopted each other." He placed a blanket over his brother's bare legs and helped him scoot his chair fully under the old wooden kitchen table. "She knows you're crippled, but she's a lady and shouldn't see you like this."

"Who is she?"

Nerrin began straightening up the small place. "You'll see."

~~~~~~

Dorian placed the baskets of food on the ground, then set Aurora's baskets to the side.

"Don't cry." He drew her into his body. "Where are you from?"

"It's just so sad." She leaned on his shoulder. "Why are those children made to work so hard in the fields? Did you see that old bastard yelling and hitting them? I wanted to break his neck. Where are

113

the parents?" The sewage smell made her almost as sick as seeing the treatment of the children.

He stroked the side of her face. "Why don't you know about our life?" he whispered.

"I'm not from here. Tell me about the life here." She looked around the shantytown. "Is this how people live?" She wanted to throw up. *This* must have been what Somian was talking about.

"Excluding the soldiers. There are three classes of people. At the bottom are the laborers. They work in the factories and their children work in the fields. In exchange for their service, they are given a two-room shack, two meals a day and one bit a week."

"Each working member of the family receives a bit per week, or each family?" She wiped off her face and straightened her dress. She didn't want Nerrin seeing her like this.

"A bit per member. When you do not work, you are not fed or paid, so children are put to work at an early age. The boy in here is a cripple. His family will have to share their food with him unless they find a job he can do like weaving baskets, making jewelry, clothing."

She shook her head. "This is horrible. Why do they stay?"

He pointed to the distant woods. "And go where? Prophious has trolls and his creatures out there. The only things keeping us safe are the soldiers." He shrugged. "I shouldn't even be here. If the mayor of the city found out, my business would be taken from me. I'd be forced to live out here as a laborer."

Eyes widened from horror, she said, "I had no idea. You shouldn't have come."

"I know what I'm doing. The soldiers are the only ones allowed to come here. They give clothing and food to the laborers, but Prophious doesn't like it. They keep it to a minimum to keep him from harming the laborers."

She couldn't believe her ears. "This is messed up."

He nodded in agreement. "I'm a merchant. The soldiers bring the goods from the laborers to us. We sell them in our stores or in the market. I'm allowed to keep one fourth of the profit. The rest goes to the governor of the province. The governor, in turn, pays Prophious."

"And what of those people who shop in your stores? Where are they coming from?"

"No one knows. It's as if they appear out of thin air every morning and disappear every evening."

A portal. But to where is the question. "Laborers, merchants, soldiers, and the government."

"Yes. Prophious is in charge of the government. When I was a child, the realm was at war, and this system is the closest to peace the realm could come. Prophious won in many ways, but the military never fully supported him. And he knows this. The military is in an odd position. They are going along with Prophious because he is a powerful sorcerer, yet protecting us as much as they can. They await their leader's return."

Nerrin peeked his head outside. "I'm all done. You can come in now."

She and Dorian went inside and set the baskets on the kitchen table.

"I'm sorry to disturb you. I'm Aurora." She held her hand out to the confused teen. "I met Nerrin in the market. And this is my friend Dorian."

"I'm Jon." He nodded. "We're grateful, but why have you done this?" He motioned toward the baskets. "How will we ever repay you?"

Her lips rolled into a mischievous grin. "Nerrin is my brother." She winked at the little boy, then took a seat in one of the rickety ladder-back chairs. "Tomorrow I'm bringing my friend here. He is Commander Tahlan and has returned to lead his troops to victory over Prophious. He'll not allow things to remain as they have."

Dorian stumbled over a molecule. "Commander Tahlan has returned?" His voice rose with enthusiasm. "He's finally returned. Where is he?"

She'd told him she intended on marrying Tahlan, so why would he ask where he was? She smiled internally. Everyone would think Tahlan was around seventy years old, not the strong young man she rode into town with.

"Is Tahlan a popular name in these parts?" she asked.

Dorian's head tilted to the side. "Yes," he answered slowly. "This was his father's province. I'd say at least ten percent of the males are named after the great commander Tahlan. Why?"

"I just noticed there are a lot of Tahlan's is all." She wrapped her arms around her body for additional heat. It didn't work. "The commander has returned, but don't tell anyone yet. I'm telling you all because I know you can be trusted, and we need allies. He'll want to speak with your father, Jon."

Nerrin searched through one of the baskets for the candy. "I won't tell nobody. If they ask, I'll say you're my sister. I bet Jon made your dress." He found the chocolate, then hopped out of his seat and took her hand. "Your hands are cold." He rolled up her left sleeve and pointed at the tag. "Yep. That's his mark. He make more money than me and Dad put together. When he finishes growing up, he'll be able to pick a good wife. Maybe one like you, Aurora."

She gently pinched his chin. She'd bet the children didn't attend school either. "You're too young to be talking about wives." She readied herself to leave. "I'll return tomorrow with Commander Tahlan. Share the food with your neighbors, but do not tell them about the commander's return. We'll bring more food tomorrow."

"But I don't want you to leave." Nerrin pouted. "Can I at least walk to the edge with you?"

"Yes. But I want you to stay away from the fields. Do not go back there." She opened her pouch and took out three silver and one gold piece. "Hide these somewhere for your father."

Nerrin held them out for Jon to see. "Look at how sparkly they are. We're rich." He ran into the back room and returned a few minutes later. "I'm ready to go now."

"It was nice meeting you, Jon." She bowed and left. "I don't want you going into town either, Nerrin. The man in the market will be looking for you." She held his hand as they walked through the shantytown. She watched, with longing, as he playfully kicked at the wildflowers.

"Wait till I tell my dad about you. He won't believe it."

Dorian took her free hand. "I'll alert the merchants that our day has come. We've been awaiting this day."

"Don't tell them about Commander Tahlan. As I've said, I don't know what he wants to do." She knelt next to Nerrin. "I want you to return to your brother now. Remember what I told you. Do not go back to the fields, and do not go into town."

"I won't." Nerrin waved as he walked away. "I'll see you tomorrow."

"Tomorrow, little man." She and Dorian walked across the field toward the town. "I can't remember how to get to Somian's place. Do you know where the magic shop is?"

Dorian stopped mid-stride. "You know Oracle Somian?"

"I met him yesterday. He's supposed to be keeping me out of trouble this afternoon."

He laughed. "I think it's too late for that. I'll show you the way, then I must return to the market."

"Thanks for helping me deliver the baskets. I won't endanger you again."

"I wanted to help." He led her along the boulevard past the onlookers. "The magic shop is just down the way."

She looked along the row of shops and saw the magic shop's overhang. "I think I'll walk the rest of the way on my own. Thanks for all of the help. Will you be at the inn tonight?"

"I should be. If you're performing tonight, I'll definitely be there."

"I'm afraid Tahlan has forbidden me from dancing for other men after last night. I hope to see you there, though."

She walked to the shop with the intention of asking Somian for a way to make her own heat. Lamir had said she'd be able to make her own heat, but something was wrong. She was freezing and starting to feel weak.

She sat on the bench outside of the magic shop and concentrated on Lamir as hard as she could. She brought forward the image of him on the beach. She saw him expand his wings, then everything went red in her mind's eye, and a loud ringing replaced the sounds of the town's streets. Fire engine sirens were quieter than this ringing.

"You're hurting me," she said aloud, covered her ears and tried to break the link.

A young man stopped before her. "Are you alright, ma'am?"

She tried to focus on him, but only saw shades of red. She tried to hear him, but only heard the ringing. "Ah, I…fine."

He watched her a few more seconds before he moved on.

She drew her arms over her head and squeezed to keep her brain from exploding from the pressure.

You are cold, Lamir's voice boomed. Tears streamed down her face. *I can not hear you, but I feel you. Go to Tahlan for heat. I must stay away until the time is right. Tahlan will keep you safe.*

The ringing and pain stopped with Lamir's last word. Her vision slowly returned. She inhaled and exhaled deeply. "All righty then. Last time I'll try that."

~~~~~~

Somian chuckled. "This is much more than a pretty stick, Aurora." He held the wooden staff before her. "This belonged to the queen. She was a natural, and her abilities were far greater than anyone knew." He touched the staff. "Her sign was earth."

"Then why didn't she stop Prophious, and why can he control birds when they are air?" Eyes closed, she ran her hand along the deep twists of the carved mahogany. "Heat's coming from the staff. It feels wonderful." She absorbed the heat in hopes it would hold her until Tahlan returned.

"No one knew of the queen's true power except the king. She was a very loving person and wouldn't harm a soul, so Prophious took advantage of this. And he has the ability to cast spells to temporarily control the wind and some birds, but he can not control the element." He paused. "The staff is yours."

"Oh no." She handed it back to him. "You've already given me her book. I'm not taking this. No way. I just need a little heat."

"She wanted you to have these things, Aurora. I was to hold them for you and show you how to use them."

Her head tilted to the side. "So you know who I am? Who am I?"

"You are Aurora, the—"

"—dawn of a new day," she dryly finished. "If I hear that one more time, I think I'll throw up."

He chuckled and paged through the queen's book.

"Why couldn't you tell me about the prophecy, and what part did I miss? You can't make me believe you don't know the whole story. Spill the beans, Somian."

He glanced up momentarily. "You wouldn't have met the laborers had I told you. You need to learn for yourself in order to fully understand. And I don't know everything that will happen." He touched the staff. "Look at me, Aurora." He gazed into her soft auburn eyes. They'd grown darker already. Before long she'd be ready. "You're the dawn of a new day, and soon Prophious will wake and know most of the past. Be patient."

"Somian." She sighed. "You know I love you, but would you please stop talking in riddles? My attention span isn't long enough for this. Cut to the chase. Why does Prophious care about me? Tahlan is the leader of the military, not me. My role was to arrive. I'm here now. Once this fight is over, I'm marrying Tahlan and living happily ever after."

He laughed affectionately and tapped her hand. "My dear, dear child. You have a much larger role. You are the key. All of the armies in the realm combined could not defeat Prophious, no matter how great their leader. You are the one who will bring Prophious's reign to an end. Tahlan is your protector, for without you, Prophious cannot be defeated."

She stood quickly with her hands on her hips. "Are you out your flip tippin' mind?" She paced about the parlor, which was located at the back of the magic shop. "How in the heck am I supposed to stop Prophious? You've read the prophecy wrong or something."

"Come and sit with me, Aurora."

She shook her hands. "You have me too riled up now. I'm not the dawn of a new day. I'm a crazy woman who thinks geese talk. Send me back to the insane asylum, because this place is too whacked out for me."

"I understand this is a lot for you to absorb, but you must try. Soon Prophious will be able to sense you. You have much to learn in little time."

She pulled up a ladder-back chair next to his. "And how am I supposed to destroy Prophious? Y'all have been battling against him for almost forty years. You're not Yoda, and I sure as heck ain't no Luke Skywalker."

"You are a natural, Aurora."

"A natural what? Nut," she murmured.

"I knew you would be a natural, but this morning Tahlan confirmed it for me. He told me about the incident at the stream." Her brows drew in, nose scrunched and shoulders hunched. He continued, "Think back. He said you were showing him a fish call when the fish jumped out of the stream. You thought he was throwing rocks. Wasn't that an awful lot of splash? And horses don't fly, Aurora. You did it. You were also levitating to his cave when he first saw you."

She slowly lowered her head into her palms. "This can not be good for me. Does Prophious know where I am?"

"He can only sense you when you use your magic. You haven't used it since you left the woods. I'm hoping he thought you were an elf and didn't look."

"Aurora," Tahlan called as he entered the shop.

"We're in the back. Lock the door," Somian answered.

Aurora didn't feel like moving. She had too much to think about. She went to a corner with her staff and book to be alone.

"You told her about the prophecy," Tahlan whispered.

"Give her time to accept her destiny." Somian led Tahlan into the kitchen. "Tell me where you've been all of these years, and how did you stay young?"

They sat together at the table, and Tahlan told him of the other realm and how he met Aurora.

"Something went wrong. The queen meant to send you, Aurora, and Lamir to the realm where these visitors come from. It's basically the same as our realm, without the magic. You and Lamir were supposed to raise Aurora. Lamir would nurture her magic side and you would make her a warrior. Then when Aurora was strong enough, she'd open the portal, and you would all return."

"There was definitely a mistake. All I remember is the king summoning me, then I hatched."

Somian broke out in laughter. Tahlan soon joined him.

"Prophious had his men searching the visitor's realm for the past twenty-some odd years for you all. He knew you were either hiding there or with the elves. Boy, would he be angry if he knew the truth."

Tahlan glanced toward the parlor. "I can't allow Aurora to take on Prophious. We didn't train her. He'll kill her. I'll kill him myself."

"I know how you feel about her, but she must be allowed to fulfill her destiny."

"This whole thing was planned. It isn't a prophecy."

"Yes it is. I didn't tell of the prophecy. Oracle Delanda did, and she knew nothing of the queen's plan. Delanda confided in me, asking if she should tell Prophious. At the time, you'd been gone at least nine years, so I thought you were safe. I told her to tell him what she felt was right because I knew he would kill her if she didn't. He forbid her from telling anyone else of the prophecy."

"There has to be a different way."

"There is more to the prophecy. Part that I don't know. Delanda carried it to her grave years ago. I've been trying to see the prophecy myself but only catch glimpses. I see you, in fire… as fire. I can't explain."

He shrugged. "Nothing that will help you. Bring Aurora by tomorrow. I will teach her as much as I can about Prophious."

Tahlan massaged his temples. "This whole thing's a mess." He leaned his large body forward and rested his elbows on the wooden table. "Is there a way to send word to the other commanders and the general that I've returned, without Prophious finding out?"

"There is a way. And I guess I should be the first to congratulate you on your promotion."

"What promotion?"

"A few years after you left, Prophious had General Harlow assassinated. The remaining commanders promoted you to general and await your return. Prophious didn't object because he assumed you were dead and thought this would keep the military from becoming one solid force again."

"I can't believe the military didn't split."

A sly grin crossed Somian's face. "Prophious didn't know I'd spoken with the military commanders and told them why you'd left. They kept the military strong and didn't allow it to split into separate organizations. Years later, Prophious learned of the prophecy, but he was too late. He couldn't split the military, so his only alternative was to find you first."

Overwhelmed, Tahlan couldn't find words to express his feelings. Honor accompanied with a strange terror simmered in his core. Honored the men believed in him, terrified the fate of the realm rested on his shoulders. He couldn't fail them. He couldn't fail Aurora.

"Would you please inform the commanders of my return? I will contact them tomorrow with our next move? You have two days to school Aurora, then we must leave. Once word of my return leaks, Prophious will surely come after her."

"Aurora is in love with you. You should marry her now. It will make your bond stronger."

Tahlan expelled a long breath. "She's gotten to you already? We are headed into battle, where love gets you killed. She is a fine woman, but I am a warrior. The sooner she comes to terms with this simple fact, the better for us all."

"You are making a huge mistake my friend."

CHAPTER THIRTEEN

Aurora played at cutting her roast. "After we eat, would you mind giving me some heat? I'm not feeling too well." She raked her green beans with her fork. "It shouldn't take long. Then you can come back down here if you'd like."

Tahlan raised a concerned brow. "You don't have to do this, Aurora. I'll find another way." He held out his arms. "Sit with me. I wish to give you heat."

She looked around at the men pretending like they weren't watching their table. "In front of everyone? You need to eat. I can wait."

"I don't care who watches." He stood, picked her up and sat her in his lap as he returned to his seat. "After you eat," he stuffed a forkful of beans in her mouth, "we will return to our room, and I shall warm you properly." He kissed her neck, warming a coil in the center of her core.

She rested her head on his shoulder while he finished his meal. "Today has been the most draining day of my life," she murmured.

He patted her back. "I know, my little elf." She buried her face into the crook of his neck and cried softly. He pushed his plate away and carried her to their room.

He laid her on the bed, untied her slippers, then pulled them off and tossed them to the side. "I won't permit you to sacrifice yourself, Aurora. The queen

made a mistake that could get you killed. Roll over."
She rolled onto her stomach, and he unfastened her dress.

She stood then, to his surprise, unlaced his boots and tossed them to the side. She stripped down to her matching satin yellow panties and bra, then helped him undress down to his shorts.

He cupped her into his body as he lay in bed. "I will protect you, my little elf."

She held onto his arms tightly. "If not for this realm," she whispered, "I would have never known the true beauty of the sounds of your rumbly, grumbly voice, the music of the lute, water flowing, crickets chirping, birds singing, people talking, or a child's laughter."

"You love sound."

She turned in his arms. "I love sound." She tugged on his ear. "I love this realm." She motioned around the room. "I love you." She poked his chest. "I will not stand by while this Prophious enslaves our realm. I don't know what role I play, but I have to do something."

The moonlight sparkled on the determination in her auburn eyes, and pride beat strongly in his heart. His brows drew in momentarily; her eyes had changed colors. "Do you know what this means? Are you willing to die for these strangers?"

"They don't feel like strangers to me. As crazy as this will sound, they feel like my people." She snuggled in and closed her eyes.

"I'm proud of you, Aurora." His hand traveled along her spine. "Really proud. I don't know many warriors who would go directly against Prophious. Tomorrow, after I contact the commanders, I'll go to the labor camp. You need to work with Somian. See if he can help you contact Lamir." She felt so good in his arms, he never wanted to give her up.

He pushed his emotions to the side. "I know you're tired, but we need to talk about your being in love with me." He tilted her chin up and gazed into her eyes. They had definitely darkened from amber to auburn. "You're not in love with me."

She rested her head on his chest. "I'm thirty-four years old and know how I feel."

"Humph," he grumbled. "I'm thirty-eight, and you say I don't know how I feel."

"You don't. I'm a woman. I'm the expert on these things. You're a man and deny your feelings."

"Your logic is illogical. I don't want for you to be hurt again, so please listen to me." He waited for her to look into his eyes. "I won't deny that we have a special bond, but you are misinterpreting it for being in love."

"I'm not."

He gently placed a finger on her lips. "Think about this. You are the first person I saw when I hatched." He chuckled; she giggled.

"Talk about sounding crazy. I hatched." He grinned. "And then you cared for me. I'll always have a bond with you. You trusted me when you thought I was a goose. I trust you more than I trust myself, and I love you, but I can not fall in love with you."

"But you aren't a goose anymore. That was different. You were going by instinct."

"I was the first clear sound you heard. You'll always have a bond with me. You're in love with the sounds, Aurora. Not me. I'm just your first. I've shown you a whole new world where you can hear, where you feel you belong. We have a common bond you are mistaking for love."

"I know what I feel. I've seen the way you look at me. That is love in your eyes. You touch me with love. You give me heat." She grinned. "You had a bath drawn for me this morning. When I'm sad, you cheer me up. You love me."

He kissed her forehead. He'd planned on finding Lamir and leaving her with him, but the change in her eye color triggered a memory. He could remember looking into eyes such as hers and promising to support Aurora in the realm's battle against Prophious, but he couldn't remember whom, where, or when he made the promise.

"What I'm about to say will hurt you. I'm sorry, but it needs to be said." He paused. "We are about to battle Prophious, and we can't afford to have this love thing distracting us. We have a realm to save."

"But, Tahlan."

"No buts, Aurora. You're the most beautiful woman I have ever seen." He caressed her back. "What you see when I look at you isn't love, but lust and desire. And you are lusting for me. The lust mixed with the bond seems like love to you because you have never had a man before. You have never had anyone care for you before. You can not understand the difference."

He could feel her tears on his chest as she rested on him. For her sake, he continued. "After we've fought a few battles, you'll seek comfort and pleasure from me. We'll enjoy one another, and then you'll understand what I've said."

She turned away from him. He spooned her into his body. "I'm sorry things aren't as you would like. I can't allow you to delude yourself. It'll only cause more pain. I don't want to hurt you. This is a totally different realm. Relationships are not what you've learned. Warriors do not fall in love. No more talk of love, Aurora." He closed his eyes with a wish and a prayer on his heart—that warriors could fall in love.

~~~~~~

"Can I stay with you, Aurora?"

"Not today, Nerrin. I have a lot to learn and can't keep you entertained." They walked through the shantytown toward the field that separated the townsfolk from the laborers. "Somian doesn't have any children to leave his shop to and is looking for an apprentice."

Nerrin jumped up and waved his skinny arms in the air. "I can do it."

"I spoke with him yesterday, and your father has agreed. Once Tahlan and I leave, you'll move in with Somian and visit your family once a week. Do you remember how to get to the leather shop?"

"It's by the livery." He led the way. They entered the town and strolled along the boulevard. "Why must you leave? Stay here with us."

"I have to help Tahlan. I'll try to come back to you. Obey your father and Somian."

He looked up at her. "You not dying are you? Maybe I should go with you."

She mussed his hair. "I'm not planning on dying. But if I do, you'll be well taken care of. Tahlan gave me seventy-four pieces of gold. I'm leaving it with Somian to hold for you and Jon until you grow up. You both will be able to find nice wives with that and your father won't have to work so hard." They walked into the leather shop.

Though Nerrin was clean and had on new clothes, everyone still stared. He stayed close to Aurora.

Aurora was no longer worried about calling attention to herself. They were leaving the next day anyway. "Excuse me. Is my headband ready yet?"

The clerk answered Aurora but didn't take her eyes off Nerrin. "Yes, ma'am. My husband has it in the back. I'll get it for you."

"Thank you." She looked around. "What's wrong with you people? Haven't you ever seen a child before? At one point in time, you were all children." Aurora winked at the giggling Nerrin.

The clerk returned with the headband and set it on the counter. "Do you know what family this crest is for?" she asked quietly as she traced the small fiery orb with her finger. "I haven't seen it in over a generation."

"Yes I know." She handed the headband to Nerrin, then stooped low. "Would you please tie this for me?"

"All I know is a knot, and these are long. They will dangle." He played with the frayed ends, then tied the headband.

"I wanted it to dangle, so I can add beads." She stood with one hand on her hip and the other holding her staff upright. "How do I look?"

Her softly tanned deerskin leggings reached from her waist to her moccasins. The only feminine touch of her matching top was the fringes that hung from the long sleeves. He liked the beaded choker. It would go well with the end of her headband when she added beads. "You look like you live in a tree. Don't hit nobody with that stick," he teased.

They both laughed. "How much do I owe you?" she asked the clerk.

The middle-aged lady leaned forward. "Be careful wearing your family crest," she whispered. "If Governor Chanterelle discovers you've returned, he'll be angry. Stay close to your brother and return to the mountains."

Aurora glanced over her shoulder at the one visitor who remained in the shop. He couldn't overhear from where he stood. "Thank you for your concern. Like you said, it's been over a generation since the crest has been seen in these parts. The only reason you know is because it's your job. We'll be safe." She grinned. "Plus, I'm not afraid of anyone named after a mushroom." She rolled her eyes. She'd forgotten the clerk might not understand her pun on words.

The clerk laughed. "You're right. I never thought of that. Chanterelle mushrooms." Her husband came from the back.

"You two be careful," the husband said.

"Thank you." Aurora nodded at the couple, then left. "I have work to do. I'll walk you to the edge of town. I expect you to go straight home, Nerrin."

~~~~~~

Somian closed the queen's book and handed it to Aurora.

"Please read more, Somian. It isn't what I expected at all. I thought it was a book of magic, but it's her journal."

"The sun will be setting soon, so you need to get back to the inn. I'll read more tomorrow." He relaxed in his chair. "I feel like I'm intruding. Her journal was meant for your eyes only."

"What aren't you telling me, Somian?"

"I haven't seen what will happen. But I know I'm not to reveal your identity." He touched the journal. "She has written her journey for you so yours will be easier. Just follow your heart."

She stuffed the book into her backpack. "Talking about following my heart. The king didn't think he could love the queen though she kept insisting he did. He married her to make peace with those of magic. Did he ever love her?"

"I think he always loved her. Once they were married, he stopped pushing her away." He took her hands into his. "You want to know if Tahlan loves you?"

"He says he doesn't, but I don't believe it. I think he's using being a warrior as an excuse to push me away."

He helped her put on her tan suede backpack. "I think you shouldn't push him. He is a warrior. The more you push, the more he will fight back. Be patient and concentrate on ridding the realm of Prophious."

She grabbed her staff. "I shall try. Which way is the inn?"

He walked her to the door. "Maybe you should wait for Tahlan."

"Directions please." She sighed. "I think I know. I'm just not sure. All of these buildings look alike." He gave her directions. She hugged him and was off.

CHAPTER FOURTEEN

"How many flower shops do they have in this stupid town?" Aurora huffed. She'd passed the same shop at least four times. "I'm lost in the twilight zone."

Totally disoriented, she stood in the middle of the street and searched for something familiar that would lead her to the inn or the magic shop. Tempted to use magic to find her way, she didn't. Prophious would sense her and find them if she did.

She heard men laughing behind her and turned. A few soldiers walked around the corner.

She approached them. "Excuse me, but I'm extremely lost. Would you please point me in the correct direction of the inn?"

"I'm Captain Meier." The mid-sized forty-something man bowed.

"Nice to meet you." She smiled with a polite nod for all three men. "I'm terrible with directions. I've passed this flower shop too many times today."

"Who do you belong to?" the captain asked.

She looked into his hazel eyes, crossways. "I don't belong to anyone. Now which way to the inn? And please don't say there's more than one."

The tallest soldier laughed until the captain shot him a dirty look. "I have a silver piece for you," the captain offered as he pulled her braid forward so it would fall over her shoulder. "That should be more than enough for all three of us." His two partners flashed big toothy grins.

She knew of the woman shortage and how many women made extra money, so his offer didn't offend her. "Thank you." She bowed her head slightly. "I must pass. The sun is almost down, and I must find the inn." She looked down the street and noticed soldiers at every other corner lighting lamps or standing, blending in. "I'm glad you all roll deep. When I get lost again, the next one can help."

The captain cocked his head to the side, then grinned. "It's illegal for women to roam the streets without an escort after sundown. It's too dangerous for you to be out alone." He pointed to the lantern in front of them. "Once the lamps are lit, you should be inside. I will escort you to the inn. Follow me."

"Why thank you." She nodded and followed the soldiers down a few blocks and around several corners. "I'm getting more confused. Why does everything look alike in this place? I would have never found my way to the inn."

The captain stopped in front of the barracks. She stepped back into the street. "Now this looks different. Where are the stores?"

"This is where we stay during the day." He took her by the hand. "We have rooms back here for privacy."

She withdrew her hand. "I asked for the inn, not your sleeping quarters."

He caressed her face. "After you pleasure us, I'll take you to the inn. Otherwise, I'll have to arrest you for being out after sundown."

She hit her staff onto the ground. "Well if you wouldn't have walked me all over the realm, I wouldn't be out after sundown. Now take me to the inn or tell me how to get there."

He and the other soldiers' laughs echoed off the buildings. "Tough aren't you." He touched her headband. "Maybe you are from the House of Fire. They used to be in power here a long time ago. I'm the law of the town. You don't have a choice."

She eased to the center of the dirt street. "Wanna bet?"

The soldiers surrounded her. "Don't make this hard on yourself. We all know how to give pleasure."

She lowered her stance. "This is your last chance." She slowly spun her staff. She couldn't use magic, but she wasn't worried about these three. She'd learned how to fight at a young age.

"Take her stick," the captain called to the taller soldier.

He reached for the staff. She jumped to the side, pulled the rod along with her and whacked him on the back. He thumped to the ground. She stepped backward, lowered her stance and spun the staff again. "I suggest you leave me alone before I get angry."

The captain blew three spurts with his whistle and three additional soldiers surrounded her.

"Don't know how to play fair, do you?" she mumbled. "Jerks."

~~~~~~

"I still can't believe how old you've all gotten, Mirrack." Tahlan took another drink of wine.

"Well, you need to tell us where this fountain of youth is." Mirrack nodded his head. "I knew you'd return. I have four sons. All soldiers awaiting the day you'd return," he boasted.

"Our day has finally come."

"I was at the labor camp today. Are they all like that?"

"I'm afraid so." Mirrack sighed. "Prophious has tried to divide the people into classes. It isn't working. We're all tired of the oppression. It's time for a change. Tell me more about Aurora."

"Amazing." Tahlan leaned back in his chair and placed his hands behind his head. "I've never seen anyone like her. And when she dances," he shook his head. "No words can describe the urges she stirs within me." He closed his eyes, and a vision of Aurora surrounded by soldiers came to his mind. He could feel her fear. "Aurora," he called.

Mirrack's eyes narrowed on Tahlan. "What's wrong?"

Tahlan reached under the table for his battle-ax. "She's in trouble." He ran out of the cabin.

~~~~~~

Tah stood in the shadows and watched Aurora fight the soldiers. When he heard the commotion he ran to her aid, but stopped abruptly when he realized she was winning. He'd never seen her fighting style before. She would turn flips and use her powerful legs or jabs and whacks of the staff to inflict wounds, keep the soldiers at a distance, and outmaneuver the men.

"Tahlan!" She ducked a punch. One of the men grabbed her foot from behind and she fell. The captain took the opportunity to slap her across the face. The sting of his slap blurred her vision momentarily. The next thing she knew, the captain went flying onto his back and a large black man was helping her stand.

At first glance, she thought he was Tahlan. "Thanks." She picked up her staff and stood back to back with the stranger. "Who are you?"

"Tah." He saw the captain fumbling for his whistle to call reinforcements. "I'll be right back. Can you handle yourself?"

"Yeah, I'm good." She stepped on the back of one soldier to hop out of the way of a punch of another. Mid-jump, she came to a halt. "Ouch," she whimpered softly, and slid down Tahlan's hard body.

He held her close to his body and dared anyone to come near. "Have you been dancing again, my little elf," he whispered. She held onto him tightly and drew in his heat.

The stunned men stared at his raised ax. "Cease and desist," his loud baritone voice boomed and caught the attention of the few men who missed the rank engraved on his ax.

He pointed to the ground. "Line up," he barked.

"Yes, Commander," said several of the men as they ran into formation.

"What happened, Aurora?"

"I asked for directions to the inn, and they brought me here instead. I said I didn't want to have sex with them, then the fight started."

He grumbled an expletive under his breath. "Did they hurt you?"

"No… I'm just tired." She stood on her tiptoes and whispered, "I feel so drained. I'll be needing more heat than usual tonight."

He tilted her face upward. Her auburn eyes glistened in the lamplight. His brows drew in on what appeared to be a partial handprint on her face, and he forgot her request for heat. "Who did this?" he raged. He showed the mark to the men as he dragged her along. "Which one of you cowards did this?" He released her.

None of the men confessed. The captain stepped forward. "Commander…?"

"Tahlan." He ignored the gasps and shocked looks of the men. "Now which of you cowards marked my woman. Aurora, come here." She stood beside him. "What is this, Captain?" He pointed at the family crest on her headband. "How dare any of you think about touching anyone from the House of Fire. Who did this?"

Silence.

Aurora's eyes shot between Tahlan and the men. "I'm fine, Tahlan. I'm hungry. Let's go." Aurora pulled on his arm.

He shrugged her off. "Fine. Then you all die for being cowards. Down on your knees."

The men looked at each other, then knelt on their hands and knees.

"No," Aurora cried. "You can't punish them all."

He pushed her back. "Stay out of the way. They attacked a woman. They're here to protect, not rape. They deserve to die. This will be swift."

Lieutenant Tah stood. "I slapped her, Commander Tahlan. Please spare my men's lives."

He knelt before Tahlan.

Aurora ran to Lieutenant Tah and pulled on his arm, but he wouldn't stand. "No, it wasn't him." She gave up and stood between the men. "He didn't do it. He's lying to save these worthless jerks."

"Is what she speaks the truth?" Tahlan asked.

Tah's locs fell forward as he shook his head. "No Commander."

"What?" she fumed. "Are you crazy or something? He's not holding that ax for decoration. He'll kill you because of these cowards. What's wrong with you? Tell him the truth."

If Tah were wrong, his life was about to end, yet he found humor in her antics. "I told the truth, Commander, and am ready to accept my punishment."

"Fine. Kill him." She spun on her heels and stomped off.

"Where are you going, Aurora?" Tahlan asked.

"Anywhere you aren't." She kicked dirt up. "You want to kill an innocent man for a slap. You're almost as crazy as he is." She returned to Tah's side. "Look at him, Tahlan. Do you see *anything* familiar about him besides your both being nuts? You two deserve each other." She stomped down the road.

"Escort her to the inn," Tahlan ordered one of the soldiers. "Stand." Lieutenant Tah stood. "All of you stand. Come here, Captain."

"Yes, Commander." The captain waited front and center at attention. "Why are you allowing your lieutenant to take the blame for your men? What kind of leader are you? You're a disgrace. Take off your ribbons and hand them to the new Captain of Garland."

Tahlan set down his ax and tied the ribbons on Tah's arm. "I'll send word of my return in the morning along with your promotion Captain... I didn't catch your name."

He stood tall and proud. "Tahlan. Captain Tahlan. I am called Tah." He stared into the eyes of his namesake.

"We seem to have a lot in common, Tah. Do you know who I am?"

"You are much younger than I'd expected, but yes I know. You have come to fulfill the prophecy and lead the men into battle, General Tahlan." The other men began ooing, awing and whispering behind them.

"You are all dismissed," Tahlan called to the men, then walked toward the inn with Tah. "How much do you know about the prophecy? It looks as if everyone knows a small part. I'd love to have the whole picture." He took a quick glance at Tah and sized him up. There were too many similarities in their look, stance, and attitudes for them to be unrelated. "I'll tell you what I know, then you give me the additional portions."

By the time Tahlan finished telling what he knew, they were standing outside of the inn.

"Aurora's fuming." He grinned. "I'll bet she's inside staring at the door." Memories of her staring at him through the sliding door of her condo warmed his heart. He loved her fight.

Tah nodded. "She's strong-willed and an excellent fighter. I tried to protect her, but I arrived late. I won't fail her again."

"You look like my younger brother. Where is your family crest? Do you belong to the House of Fire?"

"Family names are no longer used. It's Prophious's way of making us forget our roots. My father belongs to the House of Fire."

Tahlan patted Tah on the back. "I knew it. My brothers have done well. Now give me another piece of the prophecy puzzle." He sat on the steps of the inn.

"My mother was Oracle Delanda."

Tahlan shook his head in disbelief. "But she didn't have any children when I left."

Memories of their times together brought a smile to his face. "How is she? Which of my brothers did she marry?"

He sat beside Tahlan. "She died ten years ago. She never married."

"Take me back now!" Aurora demanded as she burst through the door. "Tahlan." Both men stood. She hugged the younger version. "I was worried about you. He didn't hurt you did he?" Her escort saw the warriors and returned inside the inn.

Tah tilted her chin up and grinned. "Don't worry about me, my little elf." He caressed her face. "You're very beautiful."

"That's enough," Tahlan barked and pulled Aurora away.

"You're gripping me too hard, Tahlan." He relaxed slightly. "Do you two know who you are yet or what?" she asked.

"I was just about to explain," Tah said and held his arm out to Aurora.

She glared at Tahlan, daring him to grab her again.

"You must be starved," continued Tah. "I'll explain everything over dinner."

CHAPTER FIFTEEN

Aurora ignored the two Tahlans battling for her attention while she ate her dinner. They had work to do, and these power games wouldn't get the job done. "So why don't you tell us more about the prophecy?" she asked.

Tah reached for her hand. Tahlan grumbled a warning; Tah backed off. The young man retold the prophecy, adding, "The dawn of a new day was born and this daughter of magic would destroy Prophious, but only if the child of magic and child of fire combined strengths." He held his hand across the table to Aurora. "I'm your child of fire, Aurora. Together we'll rule this realm."

Tahlan slammed his fists on the table and sent tremors through the floor. The other patrons scattered. "Listen up you arrogant piece of…"

"Tahlan, please stop," Aurora begged under her breath. "We already have enough attention on our table."

He glanced at the heads turning away from his table. "I am the only one who gives Aurora fire. Your mother misinterpreted the vision," he grumbled. "I'm not listening to any more of this nonsense. He wants you. I've told you about men here. Don't be fooled by his charming ways. The only bed she will share with anyone is mine. If you want to tell me something, tell me where my brothers are."

She dropped her head to the table. Tahlan's jealously further affirmed his love for her, but it was also counterproductive. She needed her confident warrior back, or Prophious would win. She shook her head. This wasn't a video game, but real.

"You're one silly goose." She rounded the table, sat across Tahlan's lap, wrapped her arms around his neck and gazed into his deep, dark, angry eyes. "You're the only one who will ever give me heat. You're the one I love."

He cupped her face in his large hands, then glanced at Tah. "We have work to do. This bickering isn't getting us anywhere." Still holding Aurora in his arms, he stood. "We shall finish this conversation in our room."

Enraged, Tah followed them to their room. He hadn't misinterpreted the prophecy. Tahlan's breed never married. He watched Aurora take off Tahlan's boots and fawn over him. Tah knew her game. She needed Tahlan to fight and used her femininity to control him. Tah pulled out a ladder back chair and sat across from the two. He always thought old warriors' weakness was their sex drive.

"You're my family. Which of my brothers is your father? I know he's proud of the man you've become."

Aurora laughed. "You're only saying that because he looks like you. You two even grumble alike. If he'd been through a few hundred battles, he'd be just as hard as you." She rolled her feet onto the bed and cuddled next to Tahlan. "By the way, Tah, you are one handsome man."

"Well, what can I say?" Tahlan chuckled. "We have strong blood in our family. We produce strong, intelligent, handsome men."

"You forgot to say arrogant and hardheaded. So, Tah, tell us about your parents."

"My mother was pregnant when you left." He nodded at Tahlan. "She wanted your child."

Gagging on Tah's words, Tahlan stood abruptly. Aurora fell off his lap, yet recovered quickly and poured Tahlan a glass of water.

"At the time, she didn't know you were leaving the realm." Tah's eyes locked on Aurora's gaze, but he continued speaking to Tahlan. "She was in love with you and thought you loved her." She turned away and set the cup on the table. "At that time most didn't know other realms existed. She had no idea where you were until the vision came when I was a small boy. She thought you were dead. This realm you told me about only aged you a few years. You should be much older. Something went wrong. Aurora grew up there. She is to be my wife. You are to lead the military to victory."

Tahlan paced the room. "This can't be. I always feed the contra root to my women."

"She created a brew to counteract the contra root. She loved you," Tah repeated.

"This doesn't make sense. I never told your mother I loved her. Why would she think I loved her?"

Tah sat beside Aurora and gently caressed her back. "I don't know. Ask Aurora."

"Get away from me," she warned. "Tahlan." He returned to her side and pulled her close.

Tah sat at the table. "You two will come to see the truth. I'd always wondered how an old man would lead the military, but you're still young and strong. We've lived in pseudo peace for thirty years. The troops don't know real battle. We need a true warrior to lead us. We need our greatest warrior ever." Truly proud of his father's accomplishments, he placed his fist over his heart.

"By the end of tomorrow," Tahlan said, "Governor Chanterelle will know we've returned. The commanders already know I've returned. Aurora and I will travel to the providence castle in the morning."

"May I please speak with Aurora alone?" Tah asked.

Tahlan looked into her warm auburn eyes. Their usual brightness was gone. "Anything you need to say can be said with me here."

"I'm asking this as your son, not your soldier or another man."

Tahlan gazed into Tah's eyes and saw himself. "I have a son," he said proudly. "I never thought I'd…" he trailed off. "I'll be right back, Aurora. I'm going to order you a bath for the morning." He left the two alone.

Tah knelt before Aurora. "I'm sorry," he whispered. "I don't know how this happened. You should be with me. You must realize my father will never love you. Not the way you want." He took her hands into his and peered into her big sorrowful eyes. "You two have a bond I can't explain."

"It's love… You don't see it often because men outnumber the women so drastically, but that's what it is. For you, marriage is an exchange of money for companionship."

He traced her jawbone with his fingertip. "Don't make the same mistake my mother did. She waited years for him to return. She wanted him to love her, but he didn't. I'm not angry with him. He's a warrior, and she just couldn't understand."

"But this is different."

"He's a good man. But he's a warrior first. He knows no other way." He paused. "I saw your performance the other night. Not the one on the stage, but the one where he broke your heart groping that dancer."

He gently wiped her tears away. "I see your pain. The same pain I saw in my mother's tears. He doesn't know how much it hurts you because he can't understand. He won't stop taking other women to bed because he doesn't see anything wrong with it. For him it's only sex. No worse than saying hello. He can never love you in the manner you want, the manner you deserve."

"Why are you doing this?" She sniffed.

"I'm not keeping him from loving you. He was raised in a different time. We need him to lead our army to victory. This war may take years. What will you do in this time? You'll become bitter just as my mother did. The thought of him with those women spoiled her for other men." He caressed her face. "I don't want that to happen to you."

"I love Tahlan," she murmured.

He hugged her. "I know. I'm sorry this hurts you. Once the war starts, he'll leave and not look back. Then you'll fully understand what I've said. I'll be here for you and will love you as you deserve to be loved."

"After the war…"

"He has been roaming two realms most of his life, Aurora. He can't just stop. You can't change him."

Tahlan knocked, then entered. His stomach churned at the sight of Tah holding Aurora. They looked so comfy he could puke. "We have an early day tomorrow. Let's call it a night. I'll see you tomorrow, Tah." He waited in the doorway.

"I'll stand guard for you tonight," Tah said. "I'm up all night anyway." He kissed Aurora's hand, then stood to leave.

"I don't need a guard," Tahlan said, "but thanks."

Tah chuckled. "I know you don't need a guard. I'll watch over Aurora while you go out." He held up his hands before Tahlan could interrupt. "Don't worry. I'll sit outside of the room. There's no telling when you'll have another chance with a woman after tonight."

Tah's back was to Aurora, so he missed seeing the ice daggers shooting out of Aurora's eyes. Tahlan saw every icy shard fly his way. "I won't be going out tonight. Aurora is more than enough for me."

Tah nodded. "Very well then."

"Aurora needs rest." The men stepped into the hallway. Tahlan closed the door. "I need you to do something for me. Our horses are at the livery, and my equipment is in the base of the tower. Would you have them taken to the barracks? The horses are marked with the family crest."

"I'll do it personally," Tah answered. "We need to speak about Aurora. She's in love with you."

Tahlan crossed his arms over his chest. "So what if she is? That's none of your concern."

"You know, all of these years I've really admired you, but now..." He shrugged. "You know she's the settling down kind of woman, and you'll never settle down. Why don't you stop being selfish, and cut her loose?"

Tahlan used his two extra inches of height to his full advantage and glared down on his son. "You mean why don't I give her to you. I've told her how I feel. I'm not leading her on, as I didn't lead on your mother. I'm proud of the man you've become, but I can't take credit for it. I also won't take credit for breaking your mother's heart. She knew what I was."

"But she didn't accept it, just as Aurora isn't. If you loved Aurora, I'd back off, but you don't. You have a bond with her. Most likely the closest to loving a woman you'll ever have. Why would you hurt her like this? What if someone did this to your sister? I can give Aurora what she needs."

"But she doesn't love you."

"Not yet. She won't give me a chance because she's holding out for you. Look at me." He dropped his arms to his sides. "We look alike, we speak alike, we move alike. The only difference is, I can love her in return." He held his fist to his heart. "I have the utmost respect for you as a warrior, but you're warrior through and through. You can't be a warrior and in love with Aurora. You know this. I know this. Now it is up to you to make her believe it."

"You don't know what you're talking about. I'd never hurt Aurora. Someday the wars will be over, and I'll marry her."

"How long? Whores give up their lavish lifestyles to settle down for children. You and Prophious are the only two people I know who barely age. Be honest with yourself. If you continue leading her on, you'll hurt her. If you continue leading her on, she'll miss out on an important part of her life. I'll see you at breakfast." He walked away with his head down.

~~~~~~

"What's wrong, Tahlan?" Aurora caressed his face, wishing she could remove his burdens. The fate of the realm rested on his shoulders because she wasn't properly trained.

"I never thought I'd have children. I have a grown son. Tah is a good man." He grinned. "You're a good little elf." He tapped her scrunched nose with the tip of his finger. "I want an honest answer from you about something."

"Have you ever known me to lie?"

"No. But this is difficult. If you could have anything in the world, what would it be?"

She smiled. "I thought you'd ask something hard like the meaning of life. I want for the realm to live in peace and harmony."

"And what about you? Marriage, children?

She raised a brow. "Are you asking me to marry you and have children? If so, I accept."

"I'm being serious."

"So was I. Of course I want marriage and children. Don't worry." She kissed him on the cheek. "I'm willing to wait. I won't run off with Tah," she teased. "Now be quiet. We have an early day tomorrow."

Tahlan lay and watched her sleep. He'd never wanted anyone the way he wanted Aurora, but Tah was right. She deserved marriage and children. She deserved someone who knew how to love her. He turned his head and stared out the window. If he could only be carefree and take flight again. He missed the freedom of flight. For him there was no freedom.

The realm needed him to be a warrior, not some love-sick, lost soul. He needed to return to battle and feel the thrill of the fight again. He needed to rally his troops and send Prophious's army to hell where they belonged. It had been too long. He inhaled deeply. "I am a warrior," he whispered.

A light tapping sound pulled him away from his thoughts. He slid out of the bed, quietly crossed the room and cracked the door open. "Yes?"

"I'm Sara," purred the tall, dark haired beauty as she backed away from the door in her red negligee.

He fought to lift his eyes from her ample bustline and focused on her coffee eyes. "It's awfully late for you to be out dressed like that. What can I do for you, Sara?"

Her eyelids lowered slightly and she slowly licked her lips. "I've had my eyes on you for two days." She ran her hand down his chest to his loins and stroked. "Umm nice and hard for me."

A moment of light-headedness flashed though him. He glanced over his shoulder at the sleeping Aurora. "I'd love to, but I can't leave."

She leaned forward and suckled his chest until he moaned. "Then invite me in. Your dancer knows you need more than one woman to satisfy your needs."

He weaved his fingers through her hair and guided her to add more pressure. "I can't believe I'm saying this, but I can't."

"My room is right there." She pointed at the end of the darkened hall. "This won't take long." She gently kissed his chest. "I know you want to. Who's stopping you?"

He looked over his shoulder at Aurora, then glanced down the hallway toward Sara's room. "I'll be there in two minutes."

SIXTEEN

Sara couldn't believe her luck. She'd been paid to seduce Tahlan, but all he wanted to do was talk about Aurora. The worst part was, his sincerity made her feel guilty. With twenty pieces of gold, she'd never want for anything in life. She could stop selling her body to the highest bidder and settle down.

"And the crazy thing is, I'm actually in love with her."

She'd stopped listening to him, but this confession perked her ears right up. "Then why are you here with me?"

"I don't know." He shrugged. "I wanted to prove that I'm my own man." He thumped his chest. "I'm a warrior," he teased. "Don't get me wrong. You're beautiful, but I can't have sex with you. I'm in love with an elf?" He chuckled.

Sara broke out in tears. "I'm so sorry."

Tahlan tilted his head. "She's not really an elf. I just call her one to annoy her."

"It's not that," she stammered. "You have to leave. She's in danger."

He lunged toward her. "What are you saying," he roared. He didn't wait for the answer, grabbed his ax and ran back to his room.

The empty room sent chills down his spine. "No." He rushed in, snatched the wool blanket off the bed, then checked underneath the bed. Her staff and backpack were still there.

"No, no, no!"

Sara tipped into the room, crying more than saying, "I'm sorry. Chanterelle paid me." She dropped the gold coins onto the floor and ran out.

He opened the window. The streets were empty. "Aurora!" he yelled, then slammed the window shut. The glass shattered. "Damn, damn, damn!" He ran out of the inn through town to the barracks.

"Where's Captain Tah? I need him now." He paced the office.

"I'll ring his room, sir."

"Tah!" he called, slumped to the floor and leaned against the counter. "Oh my God. What have I done?" he murmured.

Tah ran around the counter. When he saw Tahlan's broken state, he momentarily froze. "Where's Aurora?" He sat on the floor beside his father.

"I don't know. Chanterelle's men took her."

"But how?" Tah raged. "Lieutenant," he snapped at his right-hand man. "Muster the platoon. We have a rescue mission." The lieutenant ran out of the office.

Tahlan closed his eyes and dropped his head to his knees. He felt a cool breeze on his arms and heard trees wrestling, crickets and owls. "She's in the woods." He concentrated on Aurora, her slow breaths. "She's asleep."

Aurora, he thought softly. *You ve been taken. I can hear you, but I can t see. Wake up, my little elf, and tell me where you are. Aurora, baby, wake up and tell me where you are.*

Fear gripped Tahlan. Not his, but Aurora's. He could smell the rancid musk of monaphs and hear their jibberish in the background.

Tahlan, my mouth is gagged.

I m here, baby. Can you see? He grabbed his battle-ax and ran toward the barracks livery with Tah close on his heels.

Trees and these… ewww ugly, smelly, hairy beast monkey creatures from my nightmares. What are they? Come and get me.

They re called monaphs.

Well make them go away!

He felt an additional rush of her panic surge through his heart. *I m on my way. I need a sign.* He entered the stable, and, to his surprise, Somian was there with their horses ready. He held the old man by the collar. They would wait an additional second to find out what side of the fence he chose. *Aurora, give me a sign so I know exactly where to come.* He could feel terror overcoming her. *Speak to me, baby. I know you re scared. Give me a sign. Call to Lamir. He ll help you.*

I don t know how.

He shoved Somian over to Tah. *Concentrate on Lamir. You re a natural, Aurora. You can do it. Lamir is your family. His blood runs through your veins. You are from his fire.*

Tahlan could hear and feel her call out to Lamir. He could practically see it.

Lamir. She closed her eyes and mind to the smelly monsters driving the wagon. *Please, Lamir.*

I'm in trouble. I need help. I'm scared and don't know what to do. Lamir.

Tahlan glared down on Somian. "You knew they were coming for Aurora and allowed it to happen. How could you?"

Somian calmly answered, "I didn't know in time, Tahlan. I was on my way to get help from Tah when I saw you running into the office. I prepared your horses for you."

Tahlan studied the lines of Somian's face closely, then released him. "I'm sorry my friend. First contact the commanders and have them protect the towns and labor camps.

Prophious will attack soon. Also, I want all of the wizard governors to be assassinated. The commanders are to take the governors' positions as they open. Leave Chanterelle to me. I'll give more details after we rescue Aurora. Go to the inn and collect Aurora's backpack and staff. Tah, were can I hide her?" He mounted Night.

"We'll meet you at my uncle's, Somian." Tah mounted his horse, and they rode out.

Lamir's voice boomed, *Where is Tahlan?*

I don't know, Aurora answered. *He can't find me. I'm in the woods with mona... monkey monsters. Come and get me before they eat me.*

Tahlan surged Night out of town past the tower with his son and two platoons of soldiers close behind. Before leaving, Tahlan ordered the rest of the battalion to protect the town and labor camp. He could feel and hear Lamir through Aurora. *Lamir, I need a sign. They can't be far, but the forest is too vast.* He stopped their advance and told everyone to look to the woods.

Lamir whispered, *Calm my child and feel my heartbeat. I am with you. My blood flows through your veins.*

With the low rumble of Lamir's every word, Aurora relaxed more and more.

Can you form a horseshoe with your hands, Aurora?

Her wrists were bound tightly with rope. The rope scratched her arms, but she made the shape. *I have it.*

Now lie on your back and allow me to help channel your energy. Keep your hands close to your body, and point them to the sky.

Tahlan closed his eyes. He could feel Aurora drawing from his heat. He could feel Lamir's powers gently guiding Aurora's. He also felt a light flow of Lamir's power though himself. A vision of an orb appeared in his mind. The dark orb began to slowly spin. He looked closer and saw a fire building in the orb. The fire intensified until it engulfed the orb.

He opened his eyes and scanned the sky for the small fiery orb. True fear strangled him as the realization of what Lamir's sign would be dawned on him. Aurora wouldn't survive. "No," he yelled. A tower of fire shot out of the woods and reached for heaven.

He could hear Aurora scream and feel her pain, then it all stopped. He felt and heard nothing. *What have you done, Lamir?* He and the scared troops rode toward the sign.

She is alive, but you must give her heat soon. I am too far away. She would die before I reach her. I will meet you at your brother's. Have your son show you the way. This time she will need external heat also.

Tahlan didn't have the time or energy to interrogate Lamir about his family tree. He urged Night forward. All he cared about was saving Aurora.

Instead of entering the woods, Night reared up on his hind legs. Tahlan regained control of the warhorse and dismounted. "There's something wrong. Look at the trees." He grabbed his ax. "It's Chanterelle." The branches of the trees lowered to the ground and the brush reached for the sky.

Without hesitation, Tahlan ran into the forest with his battle-ax and began chopping.

Thorned, wandering vines snaked their way to stop his progress. He slashed through them easily.

Tah stood back in awe. Mighty blow after mighty blow, he fully understood why Tahlan was a legend. Nothing would stand between Tahlan and what he wanted. He grabbed his ax and joined his father.

"Night," Tahlan called. The powerful warhorse trampled the brush and vines. Shock now worn off, the platoons of men joined in chopping a path to Aurora.

Tahlan could see the bed of the wagon. Not a monaph was in sight. The fire must have scared them off, but their musty smell lingered in the air.

He ripped and fought the trees and brush to reach Aurora, hopped into the wagon and saw her cold, lifeless body. He cursed under his breath. They hadn't even bothered covering her. She lay in the fetal position wearing only her underclothes and the ropes that bound her feet and hands. "I'm here, my little elf. Hold on."

With lightning speed, he pulled out his knife, cut the ropes and embraced her tightly.

"I'm sorry, Aurora." He kissed her forehead. "I swear to never leave you again." He brought her hand to his lips and noticed they had third degree burns. His heart sunk. "I'm sorry, baby. This is all my fault."

Tah made it through the thick. "She isn't dead is she?" He reached out and stroked the loose strands of hair behind her ear. Her skin felt cold to the touch. "I'll kill them all for this."

Tahlan locked his gaze on his son's. "We'll seek our revenge, but not now. Take off your shirt." Tahlan was only wearing his buckskin kilt and leather breechcloth. Tah followed his orders and handed him the shirt. "She needs heat or she'll die. We must leave now. Have your two best men drive the wagon. You ride back here with me."

Tah ran off to do his father's bidding. Tahlan covered Aurora with Tah's shirt and held her close in hopes of holding in more heat. "Wake up, my little elf," he whispered. "Call me a silly goose or duck boy." He kissed her brow. "I love you so much, Aurora. You are my heart."

"I heard that," she murmured as her eyes cracked open long enough to see his handsomely dark face outlined by the moon. Her eyelids felt as if ten-pound bags of ice weighed them down. "I knew you would save me," she breathed weakly and gave up the battle to reopen her eyes. "I love you, Tahlan," she trailed off and sank into a deep, frozen sleep.

CHAPTER SEVENTEEN

Tah chopped wood to work off his anger. "I can't believe he left her alone, Uncle." The whack from the ax hitting the wood split the air. "I *offered* to keep watch while he sought pleasure." He tossed the ax to the ground and gathered the firewood.

Harlow, Tahlan's only living brother, hid from the heat under the shade along the side of his stone cottage. "You've always envisioned Tahlan as some sort of god, but he's a man. He made a mistake, Tah." He leaned his weary, old body against the wall for support. "He loves Aurora." He closed his eyes for much needed rest.

"Mistake?" Tah tossed the wood at the wheel barrel. More pieces missed than hit their target. "Mistake?" He knelt before Harlow. "No disrespect, Uncle," he whispered with his head bowed. "But he left his post to seek pleasure. That's beyond a mistake. He knew Chanterelle was looking for Aurora. He isn't fit to lead our military to anything but defeat." He lifted his head and locked his dark gaze on his uncle's. "Mother misinterpreted the prophecy. He'll be the face of the revolution, but we must be the real leaders."

"No," Somian interrupted and sat on the log beside Harlow. "Oracle Dolanda didn't misinterpret the prophecy. I have seen it all. I also know that you, Tah, are not the one who will rule the realm with Aurora. Tahlan will."

"I know what the prophecy said," Tah insisted. "I'm the son of fire. I'll marry Aurora. His actions prove he's not fit to lead or marry. He'll never love her. I'll grow to love her."

Somian placed his arthritic hand on Tah's strong hand. "I know this is not what you want to hear, but Tahlan and Aurora need each other. Yes, you are a son of fire; but so are Tahlan, Harlow, and your cousins. The prophecy said *a* son of fire. Tahlan is more than a son of fire. He is her fire."

"I know my brother, Tah," Harlow added. "He didn't just leave Aurora. I spoke with the Sara woman before you arrived."

"Why did you release her, Uncle?" Tah spewed. "She should be executed."

"Because she thought Aurora was a woman Chanterelle wanted for pleasure, because Chanterelle cast an enchanting spell on her, because she told Tahlan of the plan even though she thought he'd kill her, because she doesn't deserve to die."

Tah's brows drew in. "Chanterelle cast a spell on her?"

"Yes," Somian answered. "It enabled her to seduce Tahlan. But his love for Aurora broke the spell. We must support Tahlan."

Tah lowered his face into his hands. "I don't know. Do you know the whole story, Somian? Where is Aurora's family?"

"I can't tell. Tahlan must first remember."

"In a way, I always knew," Tah mumbled. "I shall support my father." He rose and finished gathering wood.

~~~~~~

Tah entered the sweltering room with a load of wood, kicked the door closed with his foot and headed for the fireplace. "Has she woken at all?" He placed additional kindling on the fire, then knelt beside the bed.

Tahlan shook his head and cupped Aurora close to his body, giving her all of his heat, his energy.

Tah poured a cup of water. "You must drink, Father." He pulled the quilts down slightly and held out the water. Tahlan drew them back up. "Uncle Harlow has prepared a meal. You haven't eaten in two days. Come and eat with us."

"I'll never leave Aurora again." He closed his eyes.

"I'll stay with Aurora until you return. You need a break from this oppressive heat and to stretch your legs. The men need to hear from their leader."

"Bring the food and Somian to me."

"Somian wouldn't last a minute in this heat." He wiped the sweat from his brow. "I can barely breathe in here myself. Somian is preparing a spell of vision in the next room. Speak with the commanders, then return. They need to see you."

He knew Tah was right, but he didn't want Aurora out of his sight. "Pull her close to your body. Always keep her close. She needs to feel your heartbeat on her back. I'll return shortly."

He gently kissed Aurora's ear. "I love you, my little elf. I must leave for a bit. Tah will protect you until I return."

~~~~~~

The spell of vision allowed Tahlan and the commanders to see each other. As suspected, Prophious sent his armies to destroy the towns, but Lamir's dragons came out of hiding. With the aid of the elves, the dragons were able to drastically slow their advance.

There was only one dragon per province, so Lamir couldn't leave battle to help Aurora.

"Has anyone been able to locate Prophious?" Tahlan asked. Lamir had come to Tahlan in a dream and explained that Aurora was transforming.

Once she emerged from the heat cocoon Tahlan provided, she would be a new, more powerful being. Only naturals went through this process, but it didn't occur until they were mature magic-wise. When Lamir channeled his mature energy through Aurora, he unknowingly triggered an early transformation.

Prophious hadn't been located, but three of the seven governors had been assassinated. "I want the commander of each province to act as governor until this war is over. In a day or two, Aurora will wake, and we'll destroy Chanterelle and Prophious." He addressed men's concerns, gave additional orders, then returned to Aurora.

Tahlan placed the tub in the middle of the floor. "You look like you're about to melt." He lifted the quilt so Tah could exit the bed.

"I am melting. How can you stand this?" He quickly hopped out of the bed and allowed Tahlan to take his rightful place. "I'll prepare the bath." He filled the tub with steaming water and set additional buckets to heat over the fire.

Tahlan stripped himself completely, and Aurora to her underclothes. "While we're bathing, change the sheets." He lowered himself and Aurora into the tub. "When the war is over, you'll be governor of the Fire Province."

Tah pulled the sweat soaked sheets off the bed. "Did Uncle Harlow tell you about Sara…"

"Do not speak her name," Tahlan barked. "I have failed Aurora for the last time."

"But Sara was under an enchantment spell."

"No, Tah. Do not speak of what I have done. I know about the spell. The spell wouldn't have worked if I had no desire for Sara. I'll tell Aurora what I've done and ask her to forgive me. She knows I love only her. She'll understand."

Tah turned and sat on the edge of the bed. "You're about to make a big mistake. Don't tell Aurora about Sara. None of us will. Hell, I saw Sara. Any man in his right mind would desire her."

"I won't lie to Aurora." He relaxed in the tub and allowed Aurora to lie on his chest. "We shall marry when she wakes. It's what we both want."

"You don't understand women at all, do you? I'm not saying lie. I'm saying tell the parts she needs to know." He turned, snapped the clean sheet and made the bed.

Tahlan took down her braid. "I need to tell her everything, including who she is."

"Who she is?" Tah approached the tub. "You know?"

"Help me wash her hair." He pointed toward her backpack in the corner. "The clear, soft bottle with the yellowish stuff is her hair soap. Hand it to me."

Tah did his father's bidding, then knelt beside the tub and helped Tahlan wash her hair.

"You have your full memory back, don't you?" Tah asked.

"Yes." He massaged the vanilla scented shampoo into her hair. "I was in the middle of a battle when the queen summoned me. One second I was fighting, the next I was standing in my cave outside of Garland. The queen was in labor, and the king was kneeling beside her. I can't begin to tell you how confused I was. I didn't know of portals then." He held Aurora close and leaned back in the tub. "Rinse her hair."

Tah took one of the buckets of water he'd heated, tested it, and then slowly poured it over her hair.

"I helped Somian deliver Aurora."

Tah stopped pouring. "But the queen couldn't have children."

"So we all thought. She hid her pregnancy to protect Aurora and hopefully save the realm. She knew Prophious had already overthrown the throne.

She explained to me that she could open a portal to another realm. The one the visitors are from."

Tah began pouring the water again. "So she sent you to raise Aurora."

"She'd sent Lamir over years prior to prepare for our arrival. I raise her a warrior, and Lamir was to hone her magic. Then we'd return and destroy Prophious. The only problem is the queen sent us to the wrong realm."

Tah grabbed the second bucket of heated water and slowly poured it over her hair.

"Aurora would call this a hot mess." His hands tangled in her hair.

"Her hair is also a hot mess. Nappy."

Tahlan smiled. "Yep, a hot mess on both accounts."

Tah put clean linen and comforters on the bed.

"I need to braid her hair." Tahlan pointed to the body towel, then stood with Aurora in his arms.

Tah held the large towel out, wrapped her, then set her on the bed. Tahlan dried himself and dressed. "Make preparations for the wedding. Aurora will wake soon." He searched through her underclothes, he'd washed, for a matching set. "She'll kill me when she finds out I've been dressing her."

Tah covered her with a sheet and comforters. "Don't tell her about Sara."

"I must." He put a black set of underclothes on the bed. "Make sure there are plenty of purple flowers. Purple's her favorite color. We must be alone now."

Tah stood to leave. "I'll make the preparations." He bowed and left.

~~~~~~

Engulfed by glorious heat, Aurora floated in the center of a water-filled twister. She saw fire surrounded her protective shell, but she wasn't overtaken by fear. She closed her eyes and listened. The steady *thump, thump, bump—thump, thump, bump* of Tahlan's heart went further to comfort her.

It is time to wake, Lamir whispered.

Aurora's eyes flew open. She heard Lamir's voice, but... She laughed nervously. She'd never get used to telepathy. She leaned forward in an attempt to see past the flames. *Where are you?*

I'm on the battlefield.

The fires swirled and whirled until they formed scenes from the battlefield. Amazed at the fiery images that unfolded before her eyes, her breath caught. The sight and cries of men dying, quickly wiped out her feelings of awe.

We must stop this, Lamir. The fire returned to its previous state.

We will, my child. But first you must understand what has happened. You are no longer the person you were before. You have changed from a caterpillar into a butterfly.

She looked down at her naked body. *I look the same.* She glanced over her shoulder. *No wings.*

He chuckled. *There is no need to fear this change, Aurora. You are now a more powerful being.* He explained the effects of the metamorphosis, Prophious's weaknesses, a few chants, and that the queen was her mother.

Am I inside of Tahlan? She felt encased by his loving embrace.

In a way. I do not know how this happened. Water and fire do not mix, yet you two need each other. I sense something in him... I can not explain, for I do not fully understand.

So what happens if we're separated for a long period of time?

I do not know.

Great, she grumbled. *Before I went out for the long count, I could have sworn I heard Tahlan say he loved me.*

He is in love with you. I must leave and you must wake. WAKE, MY CHILD! his voice boomed, and the walls of the prism shattered.

~~~~~~

"Nooooo!" Aurora clamped her hands over her ears and shot up.

Tahlan quickly grabbed her before she fell off the bed. "It's all right, my little elf." She trembled in his embrace. "I'm here." He gently rocked her.

Eardrums fully intact, she rested her chin on his chest and gazed into his eyes. "I'm not an elf."

He brushed his lips over the tip of her ear. "Could have fooled me." He closed his eyes and rested his head on top of hers as he held her close. "I'm in love with an elf." He chuckled.

A bump at the door drew both of their attention.

Tah rushed into the room, then stopped abruptly. "I was worried when I heard Aurora scream, but I see everything is well." He smiled. "The preparations for the wedding have been made." He nodded on his way out

"What wedding?" Aurora asked, wide-eyed.

He pulled her out of bed. "Ours."

~~~~~~

"Noooo!"

Prophious broke out in a cold sweat as Aurora's scream tore him from his meditation.

He'd been concentrating on finding her, searching for a sign of her whereabouts. He quickly rose from his armchair, but had to stop momentarily to regain his balance. He rushed over to the fireplace. With a whirl of his hand, the smoke became a mirror into the room that Aurora and Tahlan shared.

He watched closely as Tahlan turned from Aurora and stared at the fireplace as if he could sense Prophious watching. Prophious grinned. If the girl couldn't tell he was watching, she definitely was no match for him in battle. Tahlan carried a laughing Aurora out of the room.

Prophious paced before the fires of vision. Just because Aurora wasn't strong enough to challenge him now didn't mean she wouldn't be someday, and he couldn't allow that day to come.

CHAPTER EIGHTEEN

Aurora couldn't believe she was actually married to the man of her dreams. She looked down at her violet, long-sleeved wedding gown, then over her shoulder at Tahlan who was unfastening the latches and kissing her neck.

"I told you this contraption was a trap," she teased.

He unlatched the last one. "You will never have to wear another dress, my little elf." He slipped his large hands into the dress and massaged her shoulders and moved along her arms until the gown fell to the floor. "You aren't wearing your under-things."

Aurora turned and wrapped her arms around his neck. "How many times do I have to tell you that I don't know how to put on that other stuff? A bra and panties is fine." She caressed his face. "I love you, Tahlan."

He turned his face into her palm and kissed her scar. She withdrew her hands, knowing he blamed himself for her being captured. She didn't know how Chanterelle did it, but Tahlan must have been greatly outnumbered. She sighed. How could she make him understand that it wasn't his fault? If she could only remember, she knew she could help him.

He drew her close to his body. "I'm sorry, love. I will never…" he trailed off.

The guilt in his voice triggered something within her. In the next moment, she saw a flash of Tahlan's memory—a stunning woman with long, gorgeous black hair was at their doorway.

Aurora felt Tahlan's lust for the beautiful young lady. The next memory was hers—a skinny, man in ragged clothes had a smelly rag over her mouth and nose. She frantically scanned the room for Tahlan, but he wasn't there. The next memory was Tahlan's voice—he was saying, "Wake up, my little elf, and tell me where you are." She shook her head. The images she saw didn't compute; Tahlan wouldn't leave her alone.

"What's wrong, Aurora?"

Her heart sunk as she realized Tahlan's guilt was justified; he had left her unprotected to be with that woman. The name Sara came to her mind.

She quickly scanned the room for her duffle bag. She needed to get away, to think, to figure out what to do.

"Aurora, what's going on?"

Seeing her duffle beside the fireplace, she crossed the room and dumped the contents.

"Tah asked if you wanted him to stand guard while you..." she pulled out her riding clothes to give herself enough time to swallow the lump in her throat, "...sought female companionship," she bit out.

He held his hands out. "I can explain. It's not what you think."

She snapped out her leggings. "How the hell do you know what I think?" She stuffed her legs into her pants and closed her mind to him, to ensure he was not eavesdropping on her thoughts. "You left me unprotected so you could chase a piece of ass." She snatched up the matching suede tunic. "You didn't even have the decency to wake me so I'd be alert in case someone tried something." She marched to him and poked him with her finger. "You made me the perfect target."

"Aurora, I was—"

"I know what you were and weren't! Get out. I can't speak to you right now."

"Just let me explain—"

"After I was sound asleep, did you leave with Sara or not?"

His gaze dropped from her eyes to the floor. "I'll never forgive myself."

"That makes two of us. Now get out!"

His pain sucked her in, but she fought it. She had more than enough pain of her own to deal with. She donned her tunic and pretended he wasn't there.

"I love you, Aurora." He slowly walked out of the room, shoulders slouched, head down, looking two feet tall.

As soon as he closed the door, she allowed her tears to flow freely. She fell to the bed and hugged the pillows close to her body. Images of her dream man came to her mind. *He's only a dream*, she admitted to herself. "Only a dream…"

The reality of her words and her role in what happened engulfed her. From the moment she'd seen him in human form, she'd been pushing him into being someone he couldn't be, the man of her dreams. Tahlan had never claimed to be in love with her. As a matter of fact, he continually said he could not fall in love with her, yet she insisted he was lying to himself. *Who was lying to whom? It was me. I was in denial.*

She toyed with the thin leather bracelet around her wrist. Instead of wedding rings, the people of this realm used the leather band with a combination of the couple's elemental signs engraved on it as a symbol of their marriage. The smooth waves of the water was broken by the rigid spikes of fire every inch or so. She laid her head on a pillow. *What am I going to do?*

Before the wedding, Tahlan explained that one of the only ways out of marriage was through death. At the time, she was glad that this custom aligned with her own beliefs, but now she didn't know how she'd survive being married to a man she loved, but didn't and could never love her. She wiped the tears from her eyes. He was more perfect than the man of her dreams, yet his one flaw was the one she couldn't accept. *It's not his flaw. He feels what he feels.* Yet, she still found herself angry with him: angry for his leaving her, angry for his not loving her.

The smoke from the fireplace temporarily averted its course from up the chimney and poured into the room. She stared as a portion of the smoke took the human form of a grandfatherly man in a long, heavy robe. She rolled her eyes, then covered her head with the pillow.

"There is no need for you to fear me, my child," Prophious whispered.

She slowly pulled the pillow away, draped her legs over the bed, and sat up. "Sorry to burst your bubble, but I'm not afraid of a puff of smoke."

Prophious chuckled, then snapped his finger and the smoke image transformed into a color version. The rest of the smoke returned to its journey up the chimney.

Aurora raised a brow. "Cute trick. Now go away." Lamir had explained to her that the only power these illusions had to harm an individual was the power the individual gave the illusion through fear. Heck, she'd seen every Freddy Krueger and slasher movie ever made. If this was the best Prophious could do, she was home free. She trembled, thinking that the ugly, smelly, beast monkey thingies were scarier than the illusion of the old man in her room.

He sat on the bed beside her. "I can teach you much more than tricks. You do not belong with this heathen. You belong with me so that I may nurture your abilities. In the form of a dragon, Lamir's powers are limited."

"Are people here really that slow?" she asked sarcastically. "You *murdered* my parents."

She momentarily looked out the window and shook her head. The sun was setting. She was emotionally and physically drained, and now she had to deal with an unwanted visitor. "This is unbelievable. What in the realm would make you think I'd follow you?" His head jerked back as if he'd been slapped. "I don't have time for these stupid games. I'm hurt, angry, and in a bad mood. Unless you're here to surrender, pop your smokey ol' butt back into that fireplace."

He tilted his head to the side, hesitantly saying, "We must speak."

"No we mustn't," she said through her nose, mimicking his hoity tone. She slipped on her moccasins and crossed over to the fireplace. "Stay here if you wish. You and Tahlan can keep each other company." She grabbed her staff. "I'm outta here."

~~~~~~

Totally dumbfounded, Prophious paced across the wood floor of his library. The train of his cloak dragged behind. "She's crazy," he mumbled. The wall-mounted lanterns seemingly lit themselves as he passed. "And that... that accent, that language. 'I'm outta here?' " he said slowly.

He pulled a large leather bound book off one of the upper shelves along with a shower of dust. He had hidden the book in the perfect place—out in the open. He sneezed as he wiped the lock that adorned the face of the book. He hadn't consulted the book in years, but saw no other choice. He had to know its secrets. *There must be a third realm.* That was the only explanation that made sense to him. He crossed the room with the book and settled at his cluttered desk. He held his hands over the book of the ancients and chanted, "Rham, lada, haum, haum. Lada, haum, haum, rham..." until the lock disappeared.

He gently turned the brittle yellowed pages, but the words were foreign to him, and he could only understand portions of the writings. He now regretted allowing his temper to rule him, resulting in the death of Oracle Maki. Killing him before he had time to finish teaching him this strange language was a mistake.

He'd been able to gain enough knowledge from the words and drawings to summon the air element, and he had learned of the second realm and its portals. Now he searched for this third realm and its threats. *If they are of magic...* his thoughts trailed off, and he slammed the book closed. The lock reappeared. He didn't have time to decipher this dead language.

He stood and lifted his arms to the sky, summoning the children of the air to do his bidding.

"Sharra la bama, ola mona, la bama. Sharra la bama, ola mona, la bama..."

Sharra maba al! boomed Lamir's voice.

Prophious fell to his knees and grasped his ears. "No!"

Sharra anom alo! Who are you to call upon the ancient ones? You think you can defeat that which is of me, he roared. *Sharra fanta fanta may.* The fires of the fourteen lanterns that lined the walls of the library shot up and joined in the center of the room where they intensified and hovered above the tabletop.

Prophious used the back of his armchair to help support his weight as he rose. "Your child can not defeat me!"

Sharra tomna, tomna. The fires swirled and whirled into the image of the battlefield that Lamir flew over; another of Prophious's armies of minions lay slaughtered. *You have already been defeated. Sharra yam atnaf atnaf.* The fire separated into fourteen separate balls that returned to their rightful places in the lanterns.

"You can not harm me. You are nothing more than a dragon with cheap tricks, waiting to be slain."

Lamir's laugh rattled Prophious to the bones. *You are young, arrogant and foolish.*

A cool breeze swept through the library. Prophious could tell Lamir had lost the link. In his dragon form, Lamir's powers were greatly reduced, yet he was much stronger than Prophious had bargained for.

He reached for the book of the ancients. Lamir obviously knew the language and had probably taught it to Aurora. But was she strong enough to call the ancients. He strummed his fingers over the lock. If she could, she would of by now, he assured himself.

~~~~~~

"Stop following me!" Aurora pushed past Tahlan and continued down the hill toward the treeline. The moon was full, the night air was crisp and she needed an escape from the confines of the cottage and Tahlan's betrayal.

"I'll never leave you again."

She spun toward him. "Are we speaking the same language? I need time alone. Alone! As in by myself. As in without you."

He crossed his arms over his chest. "Be mad. Hate me. But I will not leave your side."

"I swear to God, you take one step closer…"

He tilted his head. "We shall compromise. You do not leave my sight."

She grumbled a few not so nice words as she ran down the hill. One step out of the knee high grass into the brush, her ears filled with the sound of Lamir's voice. *You need heat!*

She fell to the ground and squinted. She could see Tahlan running through the grass for her. "Stay back! It's just… Lamir." Tahlan halted his progress.

You are in my head. Learn, volume control. Dang. Why didn't it hurt like this when I was in the cocoon?"

Do not focus on the enormity of my voice, feel me. Lamir paused. *Prophious has the book of the ancients.*

She rested her elbows on her knees and massaged her temples. "And?" She knew she didn't need to speak aloud, but preferred it to thinking to him.

He has learned to summon the air element.

"I already knew he could see what the birds see. I'm not afraid of some bird spying on me or a little wind."

A tornado is not a little wind.

She raised her brows. "Wow. He can do that?"

It depends on how much he knows. He tried to summon the creatures of the air to his aid.

"Aren't you a creature of the air?" Pain dissipated, she laughed. "Whew howdy, did he summon you instead of his birdie friends."

He did not do it on purpose, which tells me he is not well-versed. We must destroy him before he learns the secrets within the book.

She tsked and blew out an exasperated breath. "Why do they always put the secrets in the one place that the bad guy can get to?"

His deep chuckle tickled her insides. *Do not be afraid, my child.* He paused. *Why have you not joined with Tahlan? You need heat.*

"I'd freeze first."

You must join with Tahlan, then destroy Chanterelle and find Prophious.

She picked a blade of grass that had gone to seed and tossed it at the log, the girth of a telephone pole, a few feet away from her. "Why did you tell me Tahlan loves me?"

Because he does. He is in love with you.

She picked another blade of grass and tore it into tiny pieces. "What he loves is getting pleasure from women and fighting, not me."

We do not have time to play these games, Aurora. Go and join with Tahlan, then destroy Chanterelle—

"And find Prophious. I know, I know. You sound like a broken record. I'll do everything except 'join' with Tahlan. Did you know about Sara?"

Yes.

"And you didn't think you should tell me?"

Why? Tahlan loves you and you love him. We do not have time for these childish arguments. Do you realize that the fate of all three realms is on the line? Prophious must be destroyed before he learns the secrets of the ancient ones.

"Three?" she gasped. "So the visitors are from a completely different realm, not some part of this realm."

Three that I know of. There could be more. You must obtain the book of the ancients. Prophious must be stopped. He paused. *I must go now.*

He sounded weary to her. "Try not to worry," she said. "We shall be victorious."

The weeds on the opposite side of the log moved and caught her attention. She crawled toward the log and peeked over. An albino looking man the height of her index finger with short, bushy, white hair and transparent wings sat cradling a pale

186

woman of the same make. Tears streamed down the man's face and glistened in the moonlight.

"Have you come to kill me? I do not care."

His soft voice reminded her of someone who had just inhaled a helium balloon. Aurora lowered her head in a submissive manner. "I have not come to harm you. What is wrong with her?"

"She is dying." He brushed her hair with his fingers. "My love is dying."

"If you tell me what is wrong, I may be able to help."

After a long silence, the tiny man said, "Her wings are broken. You can not repair them."

Using the log to prop up her body, Aurora reached over and held out her hand. "May I try to help her? What do you have to lose?"

The fairy kissed his love on the forehead, then lifted her and placed her on Aurora's palm, stomach down. Aurora cringed as she saw the mangled wings. She straightened them as carefully as possible, then slipped them between her fingers to hold them in place and cupped her palms, with one hand over the dying woman. The ends of the wings poked between her fingers.

She closed her eyes then quietly sang, "Sharra to, mah, mah lo. Sharra to, mah, mah lay. Hamma to lapa nee. Kopa nay woma bo..." She could feel heat flow to her hands, just as Lamir had told her would happen. Her own energy dwindled as the life cupped in her hands fidgeted.

"It's working," she heard the little man say as she continued to sing the healing melody over and over again.

Totally drained, Aurora slowly opened her eyes and stopped the chant. The male fairy hovered above Aurora's hands, his wings moved as fast as a hummingbird's. "I can hear her. I can hear her," he said excitedly.

Praying God allowed the melody to work for her, Aurora removed her top hand. The female fairy reached for her love and cried a *thank you* to Aurora. Filled with joy, Aurora momentarily glanced over her shoulder up the hill at Tahlan, who was standing guard. She didn't want to love him, but did. A chill had filled her. She needed heat, but wouldn't ask Tahlan and didn't have the energy to walk back to the cabin. She rested her head on her arms.

"You are not well." The female fairy laid her hands on Aurora's forehead. "You are too cold."

"I'll be fine. I just need to rest a bit. How did you hurt your wings?"

The fairies hovered in front of Aurora, hand in hand. "A squirrel attacked her."

"You're tree fairies, right?" She remembered them from her dreams. "That's not normal is it?"

"The animal was not acting itself. How may we repay you?"

"I'm just glad I could help." Barely able to keep her eyes open, she said, "I'm Aurora." She drew in a belabored breath. "Please be careful, Prophious is at war against those of magic that do not do his will."

She drew in another breath. "Well, actually, he's after me, and I don't want your people caught in the crossfire." Her fingers tingled as if they had fallen asleep. "He has this way of tracking me when I use my magic. I think you should go before he starts acting the fool."

Both fairies cocked their head to the side.

"Sorry, I mean before he sends some of his creatures to harm you. He has these really mean, stinky, beast monkey thingies working for him." She wiggled her tingling toes.

"We know of Prophious and his war against the people of the realm. Word of your deed shall spread among the fairy community. We will be your eyes throughout the realm."

"How vast is your community?"

"It spans throughout the majority of the realm." The male fairy ran his hand over his love's short fro with his hand. "I shall never be able to repay your kindness, but allow me to try." He paused. "The one who watches you from the hilltop slowly approaches."

"Figures," she grumbled, but was glad he was on his way. She felt faint and would have to ask him to help her back to the cabin. "No need to worry about him. Do your people know where Prophious is? We'll need to find him."

"We do not know where he is, but we know of many places he isn't."

"How will I contact you?"

"Word of your deed is already spreading throughout the community and all agree that we shall help you in your quest, for your quest is ours now."

Truly touched, she used the little strength she had to draw one of her hands to her heart. "You are too kind." Eyelids feeling heavy and body blanketed by a chill, she lay her head down on her arm. "How do I find your people and how will they know me."

He motioned around. "Where there are trees, you will find our people." He smiled and called into the treeline. "Show yourselves." Hundreds of tree fairies flew out of the woods, their wings lightly glowed in the moonlight. "They've been watching and listening all along."

Aurora concentrated on Tahlan and called telepathically for him to come to her. The fairies gathered together in a bunch and formed a living picture with their bodies of Aurora's face. Amazed at the sight unfolding before her eyes, Aurora's smile grew broad.

"We all know who you are. All will recognize you," the male fairy assured. "We must go now, your love approaches." All of the fairies returned to the woods.

Battle-ax drawn, Tahlan crouched beside Aurora. "What have they done to you?"

"They have…" she said barely over a whisper as she drew in a breath, "not done…" She drew in another breath, and her eyes closed against her will. "They are... friends."

Cursing, he secured the ax in the leather strap on his back, then touched her head. "You are freezing." He lifted her and rushed up the hill.

"Did... you see... her?"

"Talking is good, my little elf. See who?"

"The fairy," she whispered.

"Humph, I saw lots of fairies. What were you doing?"

"I'm cold."

Nearing the top of the hill, he spied the cabin a half mile off. "We are almost there." Her body bounced in his arms as he ran for the cabin, and she remained silent.

"Talk to me. Tell me about the fairy."

"I fixed... wings. It worked!"

"Your powers are growing, but they still take your heat. I'm proud that you saved the fairy. Broken wings means death to fairies. But you must be careful not to give too much of your heat."

He sped past the stacked wood, chopping block and drinking well to the solid oak door of the cabin, which he kicked in.

Tah and the other males jumped up, ready to fight. "What has happened?" Tah asked.

Tahlan blew by the men to the room he and Aurora shared, then used his foot to slam the door closed. "You will remain close to me at all times." He lay her cold, lifeless body on the bed, quickly stripped out of his battle gear, stripped her down to her underclothes, then lay with her spooned into his body and covered them with a heavy quilt.

As Tahlan's heat re-energized Aurora, she silently wept. She longed for Tahlan to rescue her out of love, not duty. She wanted what the fairy couple had, but knew it could never be.

Tahlan waited for her to fall into a deep sleep, then leaned over her shoulder and kissed her tear-salted cheek. Visions of her slouched onto the log filled his heart with fear. He knew something was wrong, but wasn't sure how wrong and if he should intervene. He chastised himself for allowing his guilt to bring doubt into his judgment. No matter how angry she was, she was his love, his responsibility and her safety came first. "I will never fail you again, my love."

He splayed his large hand across her waist and held her protectively. Yes she'd freely accepted his heat, but he knew her acceptance came with the angry desperation of no other choice instead of wanting and taking pleasure from his touch.

~~~~~~

"No!" Prophious clinched his fists and released his hold on the squirrel's will. Through the squirrel, he'd injured the fairy, then watched as Aurora healed her. "She knows the ways of the ancients!"

CHAPTER NINETEEN

Tah brought Sable around to Aurora and handed over the reins. "Stop being stubborn. My father loves you."

"Aren't you the one who told me warriors like him can't love the way I need to be loved?" She mounted the fine mare. "I've finally seen the light. Now everyone wants to douse the power and drench me in darkness again. No thanks." She glanced over her shoulder at the barn. Tahlan would be ready to leave soon. "How far away is Chanterelle's castle?"

"A day and a fortress would be more accurate. I was speaking with Somian, and you and Tahlan must mate."

"Don't worry about what's going on in my bedroom." She frowned. "Actually, what's not going on in my bedroom, and the same goes for Somian. Love may not mean anything to you, but it means everything to me."

He backed onto the porch. "You're letting your pride interfere with good judgment. You're holding my father to standards of another realm. That's not fair. You won't even allow him to explain."

"Stop saying that! He doesn't love me. He doesn't even know me. And what more is there to explain?"

Tahlan approached on Night, his warhorse. "Are you ready to ride?"

She didn't dare look back at him. The sorrow in his voice was enough to tell her he'd heard her, but she didn't care. At least that's what she tried to make herself believe. She wouldn't be guilted into taking him into her bed and pretending they were a happy couple. "I guess so. Goodbye, Tah. Keep an eye on Nerrin for me. He's a bit much for Somian to handle alone."

"Travel safe," he said to both.

After a few miles, Aurora became more comfortable on Sable. She'd even sped her to a pretty fast pace. Hours later, she felt like she had been raised riding horses.

She watched the muscles in Tahlan's powerful back as he rode. He'd thrown his tunic off over an hour ago. How she longed to touch, to absorb his heat, but no. She wouldn't. She nibbled her lower lip.

Heat wasn't the only reason she craved to touch him. He looked simply delicious, and her body ached for him in ways and places it never had before. Her mind slipped into fantasies of them making love. They filled the hero and heroine roles in her favorite romance novels. She could feel him giving her the pleasure she knew no other could give her.

She forced herself out of the fantasyland. *He needs to put on some clothes.* Memories of the first time she saw him in human form tickled her. She'd wanted to cover him from head to toe in several layers of clothing.

He slowed Night. "What's so funny?"

"Nothing. My butt hurts. Can we take a break?"

"I wondered when you'd be ready to rest. You've done well, my little elf." Tahlan led the way toward the stream.

"I'm not your elf." She dismounted and rubbed her aching butt. She needed heat, but decided to do without rather than accept what Tahlan freely offered. She also worried she wouldn't be able to stop at accepting the heat. Ever since her last transformation, her desire for Tahlan had grown tenfold, and she could barely resist it before. "Will Sable run away if I let her roam free?"

"She'll stay near Night." He dismounted, then held his hand out to her. "Come, I will give you heat."

"No thank you. I'm fine." She brushed the imaginary wrinkles out of her riding clothes and walked over to the shore. Maybe after the war she could open the portal that would return her to the realm she'd been raised in. She kicked at a pebble. There was no way she could leave Lamir, Somian, Nerrin, Tah... even Tahlan who was the reason she wanted to leave. This was her home, and she wouldn't run away. No, she had to figure out a way to live with Tahlan without living *with* Tahlan. Then there was the heat. She couldn't go too far away from Tahlan because he supplied her heat. The proverbial rock and hard place had nothing on the situation she'd found herself in.

Tahlan fed the horses a carrot and watched Aurora from afar. He'd heard her tell Tah that he didn't know her, and she was correct. From the first moment Tahlan had seen her in human form, he'd lusted for her, but hadn't grown to truly know her.

But that's not true, he argued internally. Her favorite color was purple. Clear sound was new and exciting to her. She was hardheaded, spiritual, smart, funny and made him feel alive—made life worth living. His knowledge and love of her was what had scared him—what had made him vulnerable.

He wiped sweat from his brow. His body made enough heat for him and Aurora; thus the additional heat Aurora rejected wore on him. Then there was the telepathic link she continually forgot about. He'd seen her fantasies of them making love. His body had felt her hands exploring.

She sat, drew in her legs and wrapped her arms around them.

She must be freezing by now. My stubborn, stubborn little elf.

He walked over and sat beside her. "I know you're angry with me, with good reason." He leaned back on his arms. Her eyes had darkened to a warm brown, indicating her transformation was complete.

A dragonfly whizzed over the water. "I'm not as brave as I thought I was." He leaned back on his arms. "A brave man would have admitted his feelings for you instead of pushing you away."

He could feel her watching him, but he didn't face her. "You're the brave one. You followed a goose from the only world you knew into the unknown."

She giggled. "Don't forget the alligator I broke out of the zoo."

He chuckled. "And the oversized raccoon," he said, still faced forward. A few moments of silence passed between them. "I was afraid to go into the unknown, to admit I love you, Aurora."

Shrill screams sliced the air. Tahlan jumped up, and Aurora grabbed onto his arm. Flesh on flesh, heat quickly seeped from his body to hers. Tree faries gathered above the stream and formed into the image of a band of elves being chased across a field by monaphs and Chanterelle's men.

"It's those oversized, stank monkey-man things!" Humanoid screams joined in with the monaphs' screams.

"Night," he called, and the powerful horse came to his side with Sable following. He lifted Aurora onto Sable, then he mounted Night. "Stay close to me."

They rode away from the stream onto a field. He saw the small band of elves surrounded by monaphs and Chanterelle's men. He brought Night to a halt. "Stay here, Aurora." He drew his battle-ax.

She pulled out her staff. "There are too many for you to take alone."

"No. Stay here where it's safe."

She urged Sable forward. "You can follow or watch."

Tahlan and Night passed her on their way to help the elves. From what Tahlan had heard, Prophious had decreed all elves caught outside of their territory would be put to death on the spot.

He easily chopped two of the monaphs down. An elf hovered over what looked like a baby. One of

Chanterelle's men swung a club at the man before Tahlan could reach him, but a staff knocked the club away before it hit the man. Then Tahlan saw Aurora as he'd never seen her before. She was a warrior, equal to him in every way.

As he cut down and overpowered his opponents, she used her agility, speed and cunning to drop just as many. *She is truly beautiful.*

He grabbed the last Chanterelle man, slammed him onto the ground and placed his knee in the man's chest. "Where is your master?"

"I," the man coughed, "don't know. I swear."

Battle over, he bound and gagged the man, then dropped him into the back of one of the elves' wagons. "He will be your safe passage for the rest of your journey."

"How can we ever repay you?" asked an average sized man with pointy ears and long hair. Since elves lived hundreds of years, guessing his age was impossible, but he looked to be middle aged if he was a human.

"There is nothing to repay." He watched Aurora as she checked the elves for injuries. He wanted to finish their conversation. They were so close to making up. "Aurora, come here."

She momentarily glanced over her shoulder at him, and then continued her conversation with the teen-looking elf who held the baby. She took the baby from the boy and held it close to her body.

"I am Jarnell," said the elf Tahlan was speaking to.

Tahlan stared at Aurora as he answered, "I'm Tahlan."

"I know who you are, General. My family is forever in your debt." He followed Tahlan's line of vision to Aurora. "She is a very skilled fighter, a perfect mate for you. You will have many sons."

Tahlan couldn't tear his eyes from Aurora as she held the baby. One second she had fought with the best of them, the next she was comforting a crying infant. "Yes, she is perfect."

"But all is not well?"

"No, it is not. You should move on."

"We will, but first you and the queen will dine with us."

~~~~~~

Aurora had never tasted fish so delicious in her life. The lemon-ish seasoning hit the spot!

"Could I have more, please?" She held her plate out to Olana, the grandmother of the clan.

"Of course." Olana placed another piece of fish on Aurora's plate. "Now take the platter over to the men and offer more to your husband."

Aurora's eyes traveled from Olana over to the men who were seated around a fire about twenty yards from the women's fire. She'd felt Tahlan watching her all evening and didn't want to see the passion in his eyes for her. Passion that matched hers. Passion she wanted to give in to.

He'd said he was afraid to admit he loved her, but the love he had to offer wasn't the type she wanted. She wanted—needed—him to understand that love was more than physical pleasure for her, and she wouldn't settle for this realm's version of love.

"If I give this piece back, do I still have to take the platter to him?"

Olana smiled. "Yes," she said slowly.

Aurora grumbled, but took the platter of fish over to Tahlan. She nodded at the other males whose wives and mothers had already ensured they'd had plenty to eat, and felt guilty.

Tahlan was a good man, had battled hard this afternoon and deserved a full meal. Punishing him because he didn't love her the way she wanted was wrong.

"There are more of those red carrot looking things also. If you'd like, I'll bring more over." She nibbled her lower lip, knelt before him and placed the three pieces of fish on his plate. "I helped Olana fix them."

"If you helped prepare the maloors, I would like more. Thank you, Aurora."

A genuine smile touched her heart and lifted her spirits. She liked this soft-spoken version of her warrior. "I'll be right back."

She hurried over to the women and wrapped the holding cloth about the handle of the metal vegetable saucepan.

"What has you smiling so broadly, child?" Olana asked.

Aurora hunched her shoulders. "I don't know. I mean. I know this sounds crazy, but he thanked me. I don't recall him ever thanking anyone." She stirred the maloors with the large wooden spoon.

"Of course he thanked you. The men are teaching him how to treat his wife, just as we are teaching you how to treat your husband."

"Well, the manner lesson worked. Do the men and women always separate like this for meals?"

"No, child. We thought you two could use a little extra… help."

"Help huh?" Aurora giggled. "As long as that help doesn't include us sharing a marital bed, I'm all for the lessons. I'll be right back."

She returned to the men's fire and knelt before Tahlan. Here she was talking about him learning manners when she'd been acting like a spoiled brat for days. This was his culture. The only life he knew. Tah was right. She was judging him by her realm's standards—a realm that was unkind to her—and it wasn't fair. Yes she was still hurt, but it was time to forgive.

"I owe you an apology," she said softly and spooned maloors onto his plate. "My behavior lately…" She set the pot down, but didn't dare look into his eyes. "I'm sorry."

He reached forward and caressed her cheek. She instinctively turned her lips to brush his palm. The usual heat from his touch was accompanied by a tingling sensation.

"Look at me," he whispered. "Please."

She slowly lifted her eyes to his and was trapped in his penetrating gaze. He was so handsome, so caring, so everything…

"I'm not afraid to love you anymore. Can I love you, Aurora?"

Tears welled in her eyes. She had truly forgiven him, but she couldn't accept the type of love he offered. She didn't blame him for not understanding what she needed, but she wouldn't settle, couldn't. She forced herself to back away. "I…I can't…" She rushed back to the women.

"What's wrong?" Sherron, Jarnell's wife, asked as she sat beside Aurora. "You love the general and he loves you."

Aurora wrapped her arms around her legs and rested her head on her knees. "Yes. I love the general, but…"

Olana eased over to Aurora's other side. "But you don't believe he loves you," she finished.

"I know he loves me, but our definitions of love aren't the same. Our expectations are different and don't match up. And it hurts." She wiped the tears from her eyes. "It hurts to be in love with someone, have to see that person daily, know that person cares for you, but they don't… can't give you what you need, and don't feel the same way for you."

"Darling," Olana placed her hand on Aurora's, "he loves you with everything he is. I see it in the way he watches your every move."

"Mother, there's something else at play here," Sherron said. "Aurora, I need you to open your mind to me. Allow me to see, to understand what is holding you back. Trust me." She slowly stroked Aurora's forehead.

Memories flooded Aurora, along with the pain of feeling unloved.

"I deserve it all," she murmured. "Don't get me wrong. My adoptive parents cared for me, but..." Just as Tahlan cared for her, but like her adoptive parents, he couldn't supply what she needed. She wiped at the tears as they flowed along her cheek. "When we were home, they barely spoke to me and only showed affection for their gain."

She lowered her head to her knees and saw her pre-school teacher on stage announce the winner of the poetry contest. When Aurora's name was called as the first place winner, her adoptive mother leapt out of her seat and cheered for her baby. She had hugged and kissed Aurora on the cheek like this was an everyday occurrence. Aurora loved the attention and strove to be the best at everything.

As the years passed, Aurora became resentful. Her adoptive parents were using her. They didn't love her. They loved her abilities. They loved to show her off for their own gain. All she'd ever wanted was to be loved totally—for who she was: the good, bad and the ugly. In her dreams, she'd felt loved by Lamir. Though she thought the love she'd felt was only a dream, she preferred that dream world to her own. This world. Tahlan's world. And more than anything, she wanted Tahlan to love her completely.

"I can't live that way anymore. I need to be loved for all of who I am."

A loving warmth enveloped her as Tahlan knelt behind her and wrapped his arms around her. "I fell in love with you when I was a goose."

"Duck boy." She giggled lightly and leaned back into the comfort of his arms. "Where is everyone?"

The women had joined the men. "We needed privacy. Earlier the men helped me set up a tent for us downstream a little ways."

She stiffened in his arms. Her body craved him in so many delicious ways, but she wouldn't satisfy those cravings.

"Trust me." He blew out a long breath. "We need to clear the air." He stood and held his hand out for her. "Walk with me."

She hesitated, but took his hand and walked downstream with him.

"I'm sorry I disappointed you," he said. "Truly sorry."

"You don't owe me an apology."

"Yes I do." He interlaced his fingers with hers and brought her hand to his heart. "I love you so much, Aurora. I tried to make myself believe it was all physical, but... I pushed you away because of my fear."

His proclamation made her heart race. "What were you afraid of?"

The moonlight illuminated the tent in the distance. She glanced from the tent to him. She wanted to make love and believed his words, but...

but on the other hand, she was afraid to *believe* his words.

They continued toward the tent. "I've always been in control of every aspect of my life, especially my feelings." A sad laugh escaped him. "Then love came along. I couldn't control you or my love for you. I've never been more out of control in my life!"

"That had to be hard."

He nudged the sheer, purple curtain of a door to the side, and allowed her to enter first. A plush comforter was spread out as a pallet. "I swear this was not like this when I left." He bent to fold the comforter. "My body burns to make love with you, but that's not why I brought you out here. We need to talk."

"It's okay. You've never lied to me." She took a seat.

"But I have lied to you, repeatedly." He cupped her face in his hands. Though the light that crept through the sheer doorway was dim, she could see the sincerity in his eyes, feel it in her heart. "Every time I said I wasn't in love with you, I lied to you and to myself."

The tears flowed again, but this time they were tears of joy. He did love her as she wanted, needed.

"I'm sorry, my little elf." He bent forward and kissed her dampened cheek. "I love everything about you from that hardheaded streak of yours to your pointy ears."

She wrapped her arms around his neck. "My ears aren't pointy, duck boy."

"Have you looked at them lately?"

She wasn't sure what her next move should be. She wanted to make love with her husband but didn't know how to broker the subject. She rose to her knees and brushed her lips over his, then nibbled along his lower lip, just as she'd read in several romance novels. Titillating sensations rushed through her and passion's heat swirled in her center.

Tahlan continued to restrain himself, but wasn't sure how much longer he could. He held onto her small waist and prayed for control. "Aurora, we don't have to do this." He kissed her gently. "We can wait… until you're ready." He slipped his tongue into her mouth for his first succulent taste of his love.

She moaned and kneaded his chest with her fingers. "Tahlan?"

"Umm hmm."

"Who decides when I'm ready?"

"You do. If you want me to stop," he withdrew his hands, "I will."

She reached for his hands and placed them on her waist. "But I don't want you to." *I'm just afraid. I don't want to do this wrong.*

Tahlan's heart warmed. Aurora had forgotten about their link. He couldn't hear all of her thoughts, but this small glimpse had told him all he needed to know. He held her close and nuzzled her neck with his nose. *Don t worry, my little elf. I ll teach you all you need to know.*

Eyes large, she covered her face with her hands. "Oh my goodness, you heard me."

There s nothing to be embarrassed about. He lifted her shirt over her head and tossed it to the side. *Touch me.* He placed her hands on his bare chest. The reason he'd left his shirt off all day wasn't because of the heat, but because he loved the desire he saw in her eyes for him. No woman had ever looked at him that way.

She leaned in, wrapped her arms around him and soaked in the love and heat from him.

He lightly ran his hands from her waist, along her back to her bra and released the clasp, then nudged the bra from her shoulders. He'd seen many a woman before, but none more beautiful than his little elf.

He cupped one of her breast in his hand and descended on her mouth for another taste. To his delight, she opened freely, eagerly. She was ready emotionally, but he knew her body wasn't.

Without losing contact, he helped her lay back.
I want to make love, Tahlan.

He held her hand above her head. *We are.* He then suckled the sensitive, underside flesh of her arm as he continued to massage her breast.

This felt so good, she couldn't even imagine what the grand finale would feel like.

Moisture began to collect between her legs. She rolled slightly and took his nipple into her mouth.

Pleasantly surprised, he returned to her lips and nibbled.

Within a few seconds, her lips tingled. Anxious to give him the same feeling, she took his bottom lip into her mouth and suckled.

He moaned in sheer delight, lowered himself and took her breast into his hot mouth.

She'd swear there was some sort of line of pleasure that directly connected her breast to the tip of her passion. *Tahlan...*

I know, baby.

He hooked his fingers into the brim of her pants and panties. She lifted her hips as he pulled her final garments along her legs and off. He disrobed quickly and returned to her. She'd seen him naked in the cave, but... he'd grown considerably in a certain area.

Don t be afraid. He placed her hand on his throbbing member. *Explore.*

Still on her back, she wrapped her hand around his hardness. Her fingers couldn't quite wrap all the way around—which worried her—but the pulsating intrigued and excited her. The rhythm matched the throbbing between her legs. She slightly tightened her grip, then slowly moved her hand from tip to base, base to tip, tip to base... She didn't need the telepathic link; the look of ecstasy on his face told it all.

Her breathing became heavy with a need she didn't fully understand but knew Tahlan would fill. This was more than physical, more than emotional, more...

Unable to take more of her stroking, Tahlan backed away, then gently kissed from her lips, along her long, sleek neck, between her full breasts, over her flat tummy, along her hip, to the delicate tissue of her inner thighs.

She resisted the urge to inch down to where his mouth would suckle her. He repositioned her legs over his shoulders, then parted her lower lips with his fingers and licked the inner walls of her feminine folds. A current of ecstasy rushed through her nerve endings. She reached down and weaved her fingers through his locs to his scalp and massaged.

He didn't want to waste one drop of her sweetness, so he held her hips steady and continued to dip his tongue in and out of her.

Her mind and body whirled. She wasn't sure she could take more, then he took the bud of her passion between his lips and suckled ever so gently. Her breath *whooshed* out of her. *Oh Tahlan...* She pumped his tongue and grasped at his shoulders.

That's it, baby. He continued to indulge. *That's it.*

She pounded her arms onto the comforter and her back arched as an orgasm burst through her body. She heated internally and externally as she never had before. Even her eyes felt the heat.

Tahlan rose and positioned his hardness between her legs. He'd given her pleasure as he had no other woman before, but now he feared he'd harm her. *I love you.* He lowered his upper body and kissed her gently.

Aurora sensed his misgivings and relaxed her legs and body to accommodate his girth and length. *I love you, too.* She wrapped her legs around his thighs and slowly drew their lower bodies closer together.

As her body sheathed his, Tahlan watched her face for any sign of distress. Seeing none, he closed his eyes and enjoyed his tight, wet, gloriously hot wife. Though he wanted to plunge like there was no tomorrow, he kept the pace slow and steady. He couldn't count the number of women he'd been with through the years, but none came close to giving him the pleasure he received while making love with Aurora.

He increased the pace, and she kept with him, stroke for stroke.

A new type of heat flowed through his body, one that gave him strength and power. She tightened her abdomen as if to draw him in deeper.

Oh God... He opened his eyes and saw they were in a twister of fire, yet weren't burning and fear didn't overcome either.

"Don't stop," she breathed out and pulled his mouth down to hers.

Their setting a distant memory, he explored the lusciousness of her mouth as he thrust deep within her. She'd been correct, there was a difference between sex and making love. He didn't want the sweet sensations to end.

Her nails sunk into his skin, her body tightened around him, and she cried out in euphoric rapture. He released his last bit of control and joined her in ecstasy. Their bodies quaked, and the whirlwind of fire that encased them amplified as his seed filled her.

CHAPTER TWENTY

The fires in the library's wall-mounted lanterns flickered.

Prophious, wake! Lamir's voice boomed and shook the very foundation of the castle.

The powerful sorcerer shot up from his seat. He'd nodded off while trying to decipher the book of the ancients.

The dawn of a new day has been born! The child of magic and child of fire are one!

"No!" Prophious slammed the large leather-bound book closed and pushed away from the sixteen-chair oak table. More than Lamir had awakened him. He'd felt a shift in energies.

Lamir's laugh filled the room. As before, the fires of the fourteen lanterns that lined the walls of the library shot up and joined in the center of the room where they intensified and hovered above the tabletop.

"I cannot be defeated! I cannot!"

You already are! Sharra tomna, tomna. The fires swirled and whirled into the image of Tahlan and Aurora in their cocoon of fire.

"This... this..." Prophious shook his head. Fire and water did not mix. Only like elements could combine strengths. "This cannot be. I will not be fooled by your tricks, dragon!"

Sharra yam atnaf atnaf. The fire separated into fourteen separate balls that returned to their rightful places in the lanterns. Lamir's ferocious roar replaced his laughter. *I am of fire! My blood flows through her veins. Surrender!*

"Never!" He waved his hand and opened a portal to Chanterelle's castle. "I am tired of playing games. Tonight I take the life of your child, then I will take yours." He stepped through the portal.

~~~~~~

Aurora woke in Tahlan's arms and gazed into his eyes. "I love you," she said.

"Not as much as I love you." He kissed her lips and caressed her waist. "Where are we?" he asked softly. Fire still encased their naked forms.

"I was in a place similar to this when I went through my metamorphosis, but I was surrounded by water. You must be of magic, a natural. Somian said most naturals lose their abilities because they aren't—"

Satisfied his love was safe, he had heard more than enough and slipped two fingers into her heat. "Already moist."

"I had a really great dream."

He captured her mouth and thought, *Tell me about it.*

You were lying on your back, and I straddled you.

He rolled onto his back and lifted her, then positioned her to straddle him. *Like this?* He ran his hands along her arms to her breast and caressed.

Sort of. She wrapped her hand around his hardness, then lowered herself onto the tip and rotated her hips.

His eyes rolled back in his head as he drew in a sharp breath of air. *Where did you learn this?*

She clutched her abdomen muscles and slowly rolled her hips. *Shhhhhh. I'm experimenting.* She closed her eyes and guided the bulb to rub the nub of her passion. Her juices flowed, so hot, so wet. And he felt so good.

He sucked his lips into his mouth. *Take me deeper.*

She rested her hands on his chest and eased down until he was buried deep within her.

He grasped her hips and helped her make a down-swoop-up motion. *Oh yeah...*

Within a few strokes, she had the rhythm and was ready to ride free. He allowed her to have her way for a while, then pulled her chest down and feasted on her breasts as she ground the tip of her passion into him.

Aurora had heard tales of drug addicts always looking for the feel of that first high. She'd feared she'd have that problem making love with Tahlan, but this was even better than their only other encounter—and that one was beyond exquisite, to say the least.

Tahlan groaned. *No more experimenting.* He rolled them both over, trapped her knee under his arm and plunged into her repeatedly.

She shrieked from the shock, excitement, and pleasure of him hitting the right spot with such force over and over again, then finding new "right spots." Her vision blurred and ears rung as an orgasm rippled through her body. At the same time he cried out, and his seed shot from his body to embed deep within her.

He lowered himself and kissed her lips. *I could stay buried deep within you forever.*

I say let's give it a try.

Don't tempt me. He lowered himself and kissed her stomach. He slipped his hand under her waist and flipped them over so she'd be lying on him.

She rested her head on his chest and they both drifted into slumber…

Wake! Lamir commanded.

"Go away," Aurora grumbled and drew Tahlan's hand close to her heart. "Make the mean ol' dragon go away. I'm basking in the afterglow."

Tahlan slowly opened his eyes. They were still in the firestorm and Aurora was spooned into him. He placed his hand on Aurora's stomach, worried she may be pregnant. "We're awake, Lamir."

"Speak for yourself, duck boy."

Aurora, you must listen to me.

"I need a toothbrush, toothpaste, a bath." She frowned. "How long have we been in here?"

Two days.

"Two days?" Aurora and Tahlan gasped simultaneously.

Yes, and Prophious awaits your arrival at Chanterelle's castle.

Tahlan held Aurora close to his body. "I'll go after the sorcerer alone. I won't risk Aurora or my son." He caressed her stomach.

Aurora turned in his arms. "I'm not pregnant."

"Of course you are." He kissed her lightly. "This is only the first of many sons I'll give you, but first I must rid the realm of Prophious."

"Lamir, could you please talk sense into Tahlan?"

You must work together. Tahlan, you are fire. I am not sure of the extent of your magic.

The bond between us three awoke the magic that lay dormant within you. Aurora, you control water and fire. You are the first I know of to be a natural of two elements.

"Are our bodies still by the stream?" she asked.

You are at the stream now, surrounded by a flame cocoon. I have been standing guard.

"Did we actually make love? Could I be pregnant?"

You are not in a dream, Aurora. You are in the flame cocoon with Tahlan. Whatever you two have done in the cocoon is real.

She looked at Tahlan, then placed her hand on her stomach. "Then I could actually be pregnant."

"Don't worry, my little elf. I won't let anyone harm you or my son." He held her close. "Lamir, there must be another way."

If you two work together, Prophious will be defeated. Do not fear, Aurora. The fate of the realm is in your two's hands. The fate of all of the realms fall in your hands, for Prophious knows how to call portals between realms.

"We don't have a choice, Tahlan. We must do this."

"How do we get out of this fire cocoon?" Tahlan asked.

You are fire, Lamir answered. *You must learn to control your element. After you have defeated Prophious, I will train you properly.*

"Oh yeah," Aurora said, "You are fire."

Yes, my child, I am fire. For now, Tahlan, I leave you with this. He telepathically embedded the basics into Tahlan's subconscious. *I must return to battle. The elves are nearby to protect you until you fully wake.*

"How much longer will we be in here?" Tahlan asked.

Until you learn how to remove the cocoon. You are no longer the being you were before. You are fire, Tahlan. He waited for his words to sink into Tahlan. *The realm awaits and the battles continue. I must return to the fight.*

Aurora backed away from Tahlan slightly. "Time doesn't work the same here. It's much slower in the cocoon than outside."

"I must free us, but Lamir did not give me any information that would help. How do you work your magic?"

She shrugged. "I just think whatever, and it happens. Kind of like the fish call. I wasn't trying."

"I am fire," he said proudly.

"Yes you are." She pressed her hand into the fire beneath them. "I've tried breaking the cocoon with my mind, but can't. You must be a stronger fire than I am."

He drew in a deep breath. He didn't know if it was because of his love for Aurora, his metamorphoses, or a combination of the two, but he felt stronger than he ever had. He stood and helped her stand. "It's time to get out of here." He took her by the hand, then he held his free hand up and palmed the room of the cocoon. "I am fire."

Aurora watched in awe as the red, orange and yellow flames split into petals, then spun like a pinwheel with Tahlan's hand being the center.

"How did you think of making a pinwheel?" she asked, voice full of excitement.

"Oh, they are called pinwheels. I used to see children in the other realm on the beach playing with them. I'd always wanted to see one up close."

"Well this is way better than a fish whistle."

The pinwheel stopped spinning, then each petal elongated and slipped into the palm of Tahlan's hand until all of the flames were gone. "I am fire."

~~~~~~

Aurora knew this was not the time or place, but she couldn't help how she felt. She wanted Tahlan in the most carnal ways imaginable. *What's wrong with me?* She'd never been so out of sorts in her life.

She and Tahlan lay in the tall grass on the ridge of a high hill that overlooked Chanterelle's castle. Thousands of Prophious's minions occupied the field that surrounded the castle.

"Why couldn't he make this easy on us?" she complained.

"Don't worry. I'll protect you and my son."

"Umm hmm." Why this man never wore his shirt was beyond her. Did he know how hard it was to resist running her tongue along his shoulder blade? His back was just too sexy, and Lord forbid she see his chest.

His eyes burned with passion as he said, "I want to make love to you, but we can't right now."

"Who said anything about making love? I'm still trying to figure out why you're so much better at controlling your element than I am." *Lamir, how do I turn this telepathic thing off? Tahlan is too nosey.*

Tahlan nibbled along her earlobe and whispered, "You can not turn it off. You must learn to control it. Now stop distracting me." He narrowed his eyes on the castle. "You are of this realm, but you were not raised here. You still have difficulty truly believing. Once you completely believe, your strength will increase."

"Well, it's not fair." She kissed him on the cheek. "And I want daughters, not sons."

Face stern, he said, "Stop being difficult, my little elf. I will give you many sons and one daughter." He returned to watching the castle. "There must be a way."

"What about a portal?" Since Lamir didn't answer her previous call, she concentrated harder. *Lamir, we need your help. How can I make a portal into the castle?*

You have been practicing using your telepathic link, Lamir's voice sounded in her head.

She was grateful his deep voice no longer brought tears to her eyes. *Yes.*

Good. The more you use it, the better you will become. I am sorry, but I do not know how to create a portal. Your mother discovered them and how they work. She had not mastered them before she sent me through one.

Tahlan thought, *How far away are you?*

I could be there by nightfall, but this is not my fight. My place is in the fifth province. Tahlan, you are the master of fire. Aurora, you are the master of water. You two cannot fail if you work together. I must leave you now.

Aurora rolled onto her back and stared into the clouds. "A battle-ax and staff just won't cut it when fighting thousands of gorilla men, trolls, soldiers, and those yucky, slimy creatures. What the heck are those things?"

"Flornoms. That coating will dissolve your skin. Stay away from them." He sighed heavily. "We must use our elements."

"I've got it! Clouds."

"Clouds?"

"Yes, but on the ground as a thick fog."

He smiled. "Yes, I like it. They must know we are here somewhere, but they'd be blinded and wouldn't be able to fight us. We can ride the horses right over them."

Aurora remembered how Night had galloped above the ground. She'd been amazed that horses actually flew in this realm, then been floored when she discovered she'd been the one who made him able to fly. It was still hard to believe she'd been the power behind his flight.

Which was her problem. *I'm in this. Why is it so hard to believe?*

Her entire life she'd wanted to believe in this realm, believe it was her home, but now that she was here, a small part of her worried this was another dream. She pushed her misgivings aside and thought about their mission.

Her fear of heights gripped her. This would be much higher than a few feet in the air.

"You will ride on Night with me. I will not let you fall, my little elf."

"I'm not an elf, duck boy. Do you think they have someone scouting the area for us?"

"No. They know we are here and will wait for us to come to them. Their numbers give them arrogance. We'll wait until nightfall." He returned to watching the castle. "I spent much of my youth in this castle. It was my father's when he ruled the province. In the evening a light fog usually settles in the valley. By morning, it's usually so thick you can barely see your hand in front of your face."

"Well tonight I'll just give the fog a little help thickening up early."

"Aurora," he said softly.

"Yes."

He faced her, then took her hand and placed it on his bare chest. "I'm real. This realm is real. This is our home." He leaned forward and licked her lips. "The love I feel for you is real." He pulled her onto his hardness. "The desire you bring out in me is real." He slipped his tongue into her mouth, and they shared a passionate kiss. *The sons I give you will be real.*

Daughters… She ran her hands from his neck to his lower back.

Sons… He slipped his hand into her riding pants and fondled.

If you make love to me now, we can have whatever you want.

He lifted her as he stood and carried her down the hill, away from the castle, then set her in the tall grass. *Sons...*

"Sons it is," she purred as he undressed her and himself.

"Roll onto your stomach."

Without hesitation, she rolled over, then glanced over her shoulder at him.

"Relax." He laid a trail of kisses from the heel of her foot, up along her calf, behind her knee, lower, then upper thigh. She folded her arms and rested her head as her body began to tingle.

He spread her legs further apart with his knee and suckled along her lower back.

The weight of his hardness rested on the back of her thigh. She wanted him in her and in her now. "You're driving me crazy, Tahlan."

"Patience, my little elf." He showered kisses along her spine to her shoulders, then neck.

Her breath caught as he slowly entered her. "Ummm," she moaned. "That's it." She pressed her backside into him.

He thrust into her with long, deep, powerful strokes. If she weren't pregnant yet, he'd ensure she was when they finished. When he'd tasted her passion, he could smell she'd been in heat, and still was. Which also explained why she'd been so amorous.

Tonight he'd take down Prophious, and tomorrow he'd prepare a home for his queen and sons. The thought of life with Aurora mixed with the sensations flowing through his body as he made love to his one and only sent an orgasm through him as he'd never felt before. Each time with Aurora was more and more potent. They both cried out in pleasure as his hot seed found its home in her.

CHAPTER TWENTY-ONE

Aurora trembled in Tahlan's arms, but didn't say a word. He kept one arm wrapped around her as they rode Night over the battlefield to the castle. The thick fog made it so he couldn't even see a foot ahead of them, but knew exactly where the castle lie.

We're almost there, my little elf. You're doing great. He tightened his grip.

I'm a nervous wreck.

He nuzzled her neck. *A most beautiful nervous wreck.* He slowed Night. *The castle is directly below us. Once we lower to the courtyard, the fog will still make it difficult for them to detect us, but we must move swiftly.*

What about Night?

He will be fine. Lower us.

Night began slowly descending.

Prophious and Chanterelle will be in the center of the castle waiting for us, Tahlan continued.

Why do they have all of these men out here if they know we will get past them?

They do not believe we can fight our way through, but if we do, they will be ready for us. And they also believe we will be battle weary.

The powerful warhorse's hooves touched the ground, and Aurora released a sigh of relief.

Tahlan dismounted and helped her down.

It's too quiet, Aurora mused. *Where is everyone?*

They are near. Stay close to me. He pulled his hood over his head and held his cloak closed.

You're huge. I think they'll still recognize you.

He pulled her hood over her head and held her cloak closed. She always joked when she was nervous or scared. He didn't blame her; he was scared for her also. He wished there were a way for him to go alone, but Lamir was right. The fate of the realm, all realms, lay in his and Aurora's hands.

I ll be fine, Tahlan.

Be prepared to fight as soon as we step out of the fog.

She tapped her staff onto the ground. *I m ready.*

He took her by the hand and led her through the fog into the castle. Still too quiet for his liking, he opened a secret door in the corridor that led to the kitchen.

The musty, damp passageway was completely dark. Tahlan took off his cloak and instructed Aurora to do the same. *My brothers and I used to play in these hallways.*

How did you see?

He waved his hand, and the two torches that lined either side of the wall directly in front of them, came to life. *Much better. This way.* He took her by the hand and led her through the maze of tunnels. The set of torches directly in front of them would light and as they passed, it would extinguish. Occasionally they would stop and look through peepholes. There were only a few guards throughout the castle.

"Arrogance," he grumbled.

Don t you think they know about the passageways? She followed him up a narrow, winding staircase.

Chanterelle may know, but his men can not see or fight in complete darkness. He will have them stationed near the exits.

Where are we going?

This leads to the great room. If they are not there, then we will have to leave the safety of the tunnels and search for them. He stopped at the top of the staircase. He could go left or right.

What if they created a creature that uses echo location like a dolphin instead of sight?

I do not understand what you say. He decided to go left.

Good, then neither will they.

He removed a stone from the wall, looked through the hole that remained and saw the grand hall below. When his mother used to throw huge balls, he and his brothers would sneak out of bed and watch the festivities from their hiding spot in the far high corner of the room.

Several large chandeliers and lanterns lit the grand hall with their candlelight. Prophious was sitting at the throne and Chanterelle paced about. He didn't see any others in the room, which worried him. *What are they up to?*

I want to see. Aurora tried to squeeze between him and the solid wall. He removed a lower stone. *Thanks.* She peered through the hole. *Why do they have those lanterns and candles lit when you're fire?* The floor looked like a giant tic-tac-toe board with stone walkways as the lines and border and wood panels as the squares.

How else will they see? The grand hall is in the center of the fortress and has no windows. You forget, there are no switches to turn the lights on and off here. I would have trouble understanding the concepts from that other realm if I had not been there to see for myself.

Then why didn't they fight us outside where they'd have moonlight?

Lamir can not get to them here. He stared at the floor paneling. The center didn't quite look right. Unlike the rest of the castle, which had stone floors, the grand hall had a highly polished wood floor.

What element is Chanterelle? Aurora asked.

I believe he is air. Come, it is time to fight. He took her by the hand and led her back the way they'd come. *Prophious is challenging us.*

Two against two. He's actually fighting fair. No way.

No, not fair. He guided her down the winding stairwell. *He thought we'd have to fight our way through his army. If we made it through, we'd be weary. He and Chanterelle are superior sorcerers than us, thus he has more tricks up his sleeve. But we still have the advantage.* He stopped at the bottom of the stairwell.

How?

Our knowledge of the other realm. We can think of ways to fight they could not imagine, especially you. And they will not have the telepathic link that we do. We can sense each other.

Do they know we are here?

They know we are close. Tahlan felt along the wall for the lever to open the exit from the secret passage.

Instead of opening into a library or some other cool spot as Aurora had seen in the movies, they entered the pantry. They both felt their way around what she figured were bags of rice, flour and cornmeal to the door.

Tahlan rested his ear on the door, listened and heard nothing. He cracked the door open and again listened. Still nothing. They stepped out, and to his relief, there was no ambush.

Tahlan, this doesn't feel right. This has been too easy.

I agree. We will have to see what he has in store for us. Be careful of the wood floor in the grand hall. Stay on the stone walkways as much as possible. They crept across the kitchen toward the corridor that led into the grand hall. *This will let us out behind the throne.* He readied his battle-ax and she her staff.

They stood in the entranceway. She looked up at him. *Now what?*

This is so awkward. I ve always run or rode into battle. He caressed her face. *Stay out of view. I will walk into the trap alone.*

She held onto his arm. *No. We go together. Lamir said we must work together.*

At a loss, he rubbed his face with his hand. *Stay close to me.*

He strode into the grand hall from behind the throne with Aurora three paces behind him.

The sound of his boots as they hit the stone walkway along the wall broke the silence. He pointed his ax at the shocked Chanterelle and barked, "Stay."

Prophious stood and slowly clapped. "Very good. I'm impressed."

Tahlan, the floor… I hear something under the floor.

The older man held his hands out. "Come, let's negotiate a truce."

"What's under the floor?" Aurora asked.

Both of the sorcerers looked taken aback by her question, but Prophious recovered first, saying, "You dare question me?"

"You are the one with the answer, so yep." She slipped the leather tie off the end of her braid and quickly tossed it onto the center of the floor. The center portion of the floor rippled like a stone thrown into a calm lake. She shook her head and *tsked.* "An illusion. I'm thoroughly disappointed." *I can t believe this old coot has everyone in the realm terrified.*

Tahlan lowered into his fighting stance. *Aurora, prepare to do battle.*

She didn't see the urgency, but complied. She stood with her back to Tahlan so she'd see who came from behind, spun her staff and lowered herself. *Let's do this.*

"You have her well trained," Prophious said. "This is your last chance. Tell me where you raised her and bow down to me, and I will allow you to live as my servants."

Aurora laughed.

Aurora, Tahlan chastised.

Sorry about that. It wasn't easy, but she stifled her laughter. That Prophious had actually said he'd allow them to be his slaves as if it were an honor was hilarious. And she knew he was serious. *I'll be good. I promise.* She cleared her throat.

"Enjoy your last moments of life, Prophious," Tahlan said.

"You think because you can sneak into a castle you can defeat me?" He returned to his seat. "I shall enjoy watching you suffer." He looked at Chanterelle. "Kill the warrior." He waved his hand toward the floor. "I have a special treat for the child sorceress."

Hey, he called me a child. I'm not a child.

To him you are. Concentrate on the battle, not his words.

Whatever.

The center floor panel disappeared and large hairy claws reached out of the pit.

Chanterelle showed his skill as a controller of air and floated toward the pair.

Tahlan, can I puh-lease go after the monaphs?

Yes, my impatient elf, but stay on the stone walkways. I ll take Chanterelle.

Aurora ran along the foot wide stone path toward the center floor panel. Once there, she used her staff as if she were pole vaulting and vaulted over the pit of monaphs to the opposite side of the pit so she could see how many of the musty, hairy beasts she'd be battling.

Two of the ten beasts made their way out of the pit. She quickly jabbed one with the staff.

When she jabbed at the second creature, it grabbed her staff and pulled her forward. She allowed herself to be carried with the force and added her powerful legs to kick the beast in the chest.

They both fell into the pit—but she was standing on his chest.

Aurora!

I ḿ good. The monaphs dropped from the walls and rushed toward her. She spun her staff and knocked out two of the gorilla men, then ran and kicked off the wall to flip over them. She landed behind her pursuers and continued fighting.

In the meantime, Tahlan dodged another mini-twister Chanterelle had thrown his way.

Tired of chasing this coward, Tahlan drew from the fire within him and set the twisters on fire.

He fed from the fear and shock he saw in Chanterelle's eyes. "I see your master neglected to inform you that I am fire!" He held his ax in the air and the blade burst into flames. Even Prophious seemed shaken for a few moments. *Aurora, they did not know of my transformation. We will be victorious.*

While Chanterelle's attention was on the ax, Tahlan commanded the fire from the lantern behind

Chanterelle to jump onto the sorcerer's clothing. Chanterelle screamed and hit at the flames as they quickly engulfed him.

Prophious stood and clapped his hands. All of the fire in the grand hall was extinguished.

The lanterns and candles glowed with a faint yellow light, and Tahlan's ax blade turned to steel.

Tahlan, I can barely see. But don t worry, neither can they.

Chanterelle fell to the floor. When he landed on the wood panel, spikes shot out from the floor and ended the sorcerer's life.

"Your turn." Tahlan strode along the stone walkway toward the throne.

Aurora vaulted out of the center pit, landed on the stones and spun her staff. "Nice warm up." The soft glow of the lanterns reminded her of lightning bugs.

"Let's see how well you do without your element." Prophious waved his hand and two of the remaining seven panels transformed into shimmering black pools. A few seconds later, soldiers and flornoms emerged.

Portals! I have got to learn how to do that. She charged.

Aurora, remember the slime on the flornoms will dissolve skin.

Gotcha! She stopped short. Fighting was fun, but she had no desire to have her skin dissolved. *Why didn t I think of this sooner.* She backed away and dodged slime thrown at her by the flornoms.

Tahlan, I can restart the fires, but I need you to control them!

Just give me fire.

A drop of slime touched her hand. "Ouch." She shook her hand and continued to back away. *You'll have to work fast before he has time to extinguish the fires again.*

Prophious laughed. "I knew you'd like the flornoms."

"Sharra fanta fanta may."

Fire replaced the glow of the lanterns and candles. Tahlan quickly commanded the fires to grow and leap from their places onto their attackers and into the portals. Shrieks and screams filled the hall. He ordered the fire from the chandeliers to burn through the ropes that held the heavy metal objects in the air.

Come, Aurora!

As she ran and flipped over their would-be attackers, the five heavy chandeliers began to fall. She easily dodged them and continued onward. Two of the chandeliers landed over the portal holes.

Tahlan charged toward Prophious.

Panic stricken, the old sorcerer opened a portal. Unlike the other portals, this one had an odd energy that vibrated through the room. Prophious hesitated. Seeing no other choice, he stepped into the portal with Tahlan close behind, then Aurora.

CHAPTER TWENTY-TWO

Aurora fought through the darkness into consciousness. "Tahlan," she cried out as she woke. Disoriented, she took in the hospital room surroundings. "What the...?"

A nurse shot out of the chair in the corner. "Oh my goodness, you're awake." She rushed to the telephone on the nightstand beside the bed and placed a call to Dr. Price. "She's awake! Aurora Church is awake!"

Aurora shoved the blankets off and pulled the IV needle out of her arm. "How did I get here, and where's Tahlan?" She swung her legs over the side of the bed and watched the woman's mouth.

"You must stay put." The nurse held her hand out. "Please try to remain calm." She blew out a nervous breath. "Doctor, please hurry."

The nurse's garbled voice annoyed Aurora. She wanted her clear hearing back. She wanted her world. She wanted her warrior. "You don't seem to understand. I don't belong here. I have to get back home."

"Dr. Price will be here momentarily."

"Thank you, but I don't want or need Dr. Price. What I need are my clothes and for you to tell me where I am." She hopped out of the bed and just about fell to the floor. *Why are my legs so weak?* She steadied herself on the bed and walked on shaky legs to the window. *I'm in Hatcher Memorial*

Hospital. She glanced over her shoulder at the woman. "Where is Tahlan?"

"Your parents had you transferred to this facility."

"My parents? How long have I been here?" She caught a glimpse of Dr. Price entering the room as she turned toward the window.

"Aurora." He waved his hand in front of her. "Aurora."

Cars sped about the busy city below. Tears spilled from her eyes. "I want to go home."

"You may leave now, nurse. Thank you."

The nurse took Aurora by the hand. "I'll inform your parents you're awake."

Once the nurse left, he took Aurora by the hands and faced her toward him. "You need to lie back down. This excitement is too much for you."

"I want to go home. I want Tahlan."

"Please, Aurora, listen to me. We must talk."

Legs ready to give out, she sat in one of the pleather chairs. "How did I get here?"

He moved the rocking chair from the corner of the room over so he could sit facing her.

"You were found, unconscious, in the forest preserve near your office building."

"Where is Tahlan?"

"There was no sight of your goose or the alligator and raccoon you stole from the zoo, but there was an old man."

"Oh my God!" She drew her hands to her mouth, and her eyes opened wide. "Prophious is here? Where is he?" She used all of her strength to push up from the chair. "He must be stopped before he tries to take over this realm also." *Tahlan, where are you?*

Dr. Price studied her for a long while, then stood before her. "He had been dead a few hours when he was discovered. He passed from natural causes."

Relieved Prophious was dead, she closed her eyes and again tried to connect to Tahlan.

After several minutes of no answer she yelled, "Tahlan!"

"Aurora, calm down or I must have you restrained and sedated."

"You even think about poking me with a needle I'll make you curse the day you were born. Tahlan!" She staggered toward the door. Two orderlies appeared and blocked her way. She crossed her arms over her chest and glared at the men. "How did they get there so fast?"

Dr. Price stepped between her and the men. "I had them posted outside the door. I had a feeling you'd decide to leave prematurely."

She spun away from the doctor and just about fell. He caught and steadied her. Five floors up, she knew she'd break something if she tried to jump from the window. *I have to get out of here.*

"I want to go home." She heard him say something, but she refused to read his lips. She refused to allow him to tell her Tahlan was only a goose. She refused to believe this realm was her home. She wiped the tears from her eyes. *Tahlan! Please, Tahlan, find me.*

He wrapped his arm around her waist and guided her to lie on the bed, then he tucked her in.

"I'm exhausted. Am I drugged?" She glanced at the clock—10:13 A.M.—then back to the doctor.

"No, you aren't drugged, but you need your rest."

"I need a sketch pad, colored pencils and an art eraser. Can you get those items for me, quickly?" She propped her head on a pillow.

"If you take a nap, I'll have them for you when you wake."

She held out her hand. "May I see your notepad and pen? I need to draw Tahlan for you."

"Aurora, I've seen your goose up close and personal. Remember, you had him attack me at the zoo."

"He isn't a goose." She bobbed her hand. "Notepad and pen please."

He handed over the items.

"Thank you." She began sketching. "He's close. I can feel him, but he doesn't speak English." She could tell Dr. Price wanted to say something, but was grateful he remained silent. After a few minutes she handed him the picture. "I need you to check all of the hospitals for this John Doe."

Dr. Price studied the picture. "Isn't this the warrior from your video game?"

"No, that warrior is a cartoon." She tapped the picture. "Tahlan is a flesh and blood man. Now please help me find him."

"I'll help you look for your Tahlan, but you must promise to cooperate during therapy until he shows up."

Lips pursed, she said, "You don't believe me, but I don't care. Sure, I'll actually try the therapy, but you have to actually look for Tahlan. Deal?"

"Deal."

She began to sketch another portrait of Tahlan. "Where are my parents?" She looked up to see his reply.

"After they ensured you were okay, they returned to Houston."

The sorrow of the realm returned to Aurora. "I don't know why I expected them to stay. It's stupid."

"Aurora." He placed his hand on hers. "They stayed for two months. Your mother refused to leave your side."

"Two months!" *Time and those blasted portals! What if Tahlan's unconscious?*

"It's been almost three months. Your mother returns every weekend."

All Aurora could do was stare at Dr. Price.

"There was nothing more they could do, so I insisted they return to their ministry. Your physician will be here soon to—"

She lowered her head and continued her sketch. After several sketches, she heard the physician enter the room and say something to Dr. Price. Both men sounded excited. Her body began to warm. She felt him, Tahlan. He was drowsy. Waking. He was near!

"I need a wheelchair."

The doctors looked at her.

"A wheeeeelchair, please." She'd bet he was in the same building.

"You must be examined, Aurora. You're in a delicate state." The doctors approached the bed.

"You promised to help me find Tahlan. He's here. I know he's here."

"And I will, but first you must allow Dr. Willis to conduct a full examination."

"Fine, but while he's treating me like some sort of guinea pig, can you start getting the list of all the John Does, or whatever they call unknown folks, for me?" She wrote Tahlan's physical description on the notepad. "This should make it easier for you. Have your goons check every room of this hospital."

~~~~~~

Tahlan fought through the darkness into consciousness. "Aurora," he cried out as he woke. Disoriented, he took in his surroundings. "Where in the realm am I?"

Everything was white, and he lay in a bed with a small table that had wheels on it nearby. Clear vines were hooked to a bag filled with a watery looking substance. The vines led to a piece of metal that was stuck in his arm. He yanked the metal out.

A woman dressed in all white rushed to his side and said something garbled that he couldn't understand. He shoved the covers off, stepped out of the bed and almost fell to the floor.

My legs!

The woman fussed and tried to help him stand. He grumbled and used the bed to help balance himself, then he grabbed onto the rolling table and made his way to the window. *Oh no!*

He stared at the mid-morning traffic three floors below.

The woman in white pulled on his arm and kept clucking worse than any chicken.

He sat in a nearby chair before he fell and lowered his face into his palms. They'd been sent back to the realm where he'd been a goose. He hated to admit it, but he'd have an easier time finding her if he were a goose. In human form he didn't know the language and had no idea on how to find her, but he would.

The woman in white was on that phone thing Aurora had told him about. He closed his eyes and leaned back. *Aurora!*

"Tahlan!"

He spun around toward the door and saw Aurora sitting in a chair with huge wheels. The man behind her looked completely outdone.

"Aurora!"

They stumbled to each other and embraced. Tahlan wiped the tears from Aurora's eyes.

All is good in the realm as long as I have you.

The doctors and nurses helped them both sit on the bed.

She gazed into Tahlan's eyes. *And I am home as long as I'm in your arms.*

Where is Prophious?

The portal did not treat him well. He is dead.

Excellent.

Dr. Price tapped on Aurora's shoulder. After she looked his way, he nervously said,

"Everything you told me was true. The goose is..." He stared at Tahlan. "I'm sorry, this is just all so unbelievable." He smoothed his hand over his face. "Well, I guess congratulations are in order."

What is this man saying? I want to make love with you, not listen to him. Tell them we are going home.

She caressed Tahlan's face. *You can barely walk, how will you make love to me?* She giggled.

I'll figure something out.

Dr. Price tapped her arm.

If that man touches you one more time, I'll rip his arms off.

Be good, Tahlan. She smiled. *You're going to be a father!*

My sons! He kissed her passionately. *I love you so much.*

I love you, too. Let's go home. She didn't want to, but pulled away. "How long will it take for us to be discharged? We want to go home."

"Home being?"

"You'll see."

~~~~~~

Before they left the hospital, Aurora had contacted her mother and explained how she was grateful for everything they had done for her. That she loved her and wished her the best in life, but she was moving on with her life. Her mother didn't understand, yet understood, and wished the best for Aurora. Now that Prophious was dead and she'd settled things with her family, she was truly free to live her life.

A low vibration filled the air.

"We're getting close to the portal," Aurora said and guided the jeep toward the vibration.

Trees surrounded them on every side, weed and wild flowers were in abundance, and this time she recognized the portal.

"Thank you for everything, Dr. Price, especially not telling the authorities of the other realm." She parked the jeep between two large trees.

"I'm still outdone." He looked around. "I don't see a portal."

"That's what I said the first time."

Tahlan stepped onto the ground and held his hand out to Aurora. He bowed his head to Dr. Price in thanks.

"You are welcome."

Aurora placed her hand into Tahlan's. Since waking several hours ago, both had regained their strength. "Goodbye, Dr. Price." She waved her hand toward the portal. "Open."

She took one last look at the realm she was raised in, then stepped into the portal and went home to raise her child with the man of her dreams.

THE END

A Word From The Author

I absolutely love fantasy and science-fiction novels. Throw romance into the mix, and I'm in heaven. Thank you for taking this chance with me. I hope you enjoyed reading it as much as I enjoyed writing it.

I love hearing from readers. If you and/or your book club would like to discuss The Other Realm or any of my other titles, contact me at deatri@deewrites.com. You can also join me in cyberworld at http://deatrikingbey.com.

Until next time, keep on reading and see you on the Internet.

Deatri King-Bey

www.ingramcontent.com/pod-product-compliance
Lightning Source LLC
Chambersburg PA
CBHW070558130626
46556CB00001B/202